THE GENTLEMAN'S JOURNEY

A heartwarming story of courage, compassion, and wisdom

SKIP JOHNSON

"Don't judge each day
by the harvest you reap,
but by the seeds that you plant."

—Robert Louis Stevenson

Other Books by Skip Johnson

The Mystic's Gift:
A Story About Loss, Letting Go . . . and Learning to Soar
(Book 1 in the Royce Holloway series)

A spellbinding, deeply moving story that is destined to become a self-help classic. Following a sudden, unimaginable personal tragedy at a point in his midlife where Royce Holloway thought he had it all, he is introduced to a wise, exotic, enchanting mentor named Maya, who takes Royce on a powerful journey of courageous self-discovery and incredible possibilities. What he learns on this captivating, often poignant trek across two continents will change him in a powerful way, but you may find that the life changed most . . . is yours.

Grateful for Everything:
Learning, Living, and Loving the Great Game of Life

A blueprint for using the power of gratitude to increase your happiness and fulfillment. You'll find useful, specific tools and ideas for turning your life into a great game to play instead of a dreary battle to fight.

Hidden Jewels of Happiness:
Powerful Essays for Finding and Savoring
the Gifts on Your Journey

A book of wisdom, encouragement, and empowerment for dealing with life's daily challenges. Let Skip show you the seemingly hidden gifts that are all around us, waiting to be found and enjoyed. You'll feel inspired, enlightened, and happier as you read each and every page.

DEDICATION

To my mom, Shirley, who has never been too busy
to listen any time I have needed to be heard.
I love you, and I am grateful for you.

TABLE OF CONTENTS

CHAPTER 1

Royce Holloway sat quietly in an old brown rocking chair in the den of his Georgia home, looking out a large bay window at the evening rain. He was clutching a crumpled note he had just finished reading after nostalgically retrieving it from his nightstand drawer. The melancholy he felt seemed mirrored by the dreary weather, which had been going on for days now.

He glanced over at the beautiful bronze Indian statue on his bookshelf. The poignant sculpture of a couple standing close together as they gazed up in unison at a lone star was usually a source of so many inspiring memories . . . but now it simply added to his gloominess as Royce sipped on a glass of cool, sparkling water.

Five years. Could it really have been five years already since those life-changing seven days spent immersed in conversation with his mystical Indian mentor, Maya, at her magnificent garden-covered property? Like the last few years, that week had gone by so quickly—seven blissful days of sitting with this incredible teacher, a wise and exotic woman who had helped transform his life when he needed it most.

Back then, following the sudden death of his wife, Royce had no idea how he would carry on. He and his two young daughters knew they had to somehow figure it out on their own, and yet every day was a struggle. After twenty years of marriage, Royce had become a widower . . . and he'd had no clue as to what to do next. His confidence and courage were faltering day by day, and he was desperate for answers.

But after he was introduced to Maya by his good friend Stewart Edge, life had changed in a way he could never have imagined. Daily, Maya shared with him ancient principles from a secret book, *The Six Principles of Sacred Power*, which had been passed down to her by her father. Like the rest of the world, Royce had no knowledge of the book, which contained startling truths that Indian leader Mahatma Gandhi had uncovered through years of tirelessly studying the works of the greatest spiritual teachers in history. The Six Principles outlined in the book were those that Gandhi had discovered were common to all the great mentors. Such was their potency that when a person absorbed and tapped into those principles, their personal and spiritual powers became supercharged— and they became capable of extraordinary feats.

The Six Principles of Sacred Power had been clandestinely published at a small bookbinding shop owned by Gandhi's former law school friend in Ceylon, known today as Sri Lanka. Copies of the book were only shared with Mr. Gandhi's six closest confidants—

including Maya's father, a popular philosophy professor at the University of New Delhi. Though ironically an Englishman, he had been part of a small, select group of men working with Gandhi to lead the peaceful resistance to British occupation, and he had become Gandhi's right-hand man in the movement.

To make sure the book never fell into the wrong hands, not only were there just seven copies in existence, but these could only be passed on upon the owner's death—and only to a single designated heir. In the same way, those heirs could then pass the book on to a person of their own choosing, and by learning and practicing the book's principles, those "chosen" people would subsequently become endowed with the same seemingly impossible powers. Furthermore, anyone that spent any extended time with the owners of the books was impacted in an inexplicable way, empowered with substantially increased faith, courage, and inner strength.

Maya, however, had made it clear to Royce that these God-given "powers" were capabilities that each of us *already* innately possesses, but which typically become inactive—hopelessly buried under layers of anxiety, fear, self-doubt, and discouragement. Thus, the true magic of *The Six Principles of Sacred Power* was that the wisdom contained in the book taught people how to restore their inherent personal power by stripping away the blockages that interfered with their strength.

As the heir to her father's copy of the book, and by virtue of her father's closeness to Gandhi, Maya had been gifted the unique opportunity to pass the book on at the time of her choice. Through a series of fortuitous events, she had chosen Royce—and not a moment too soon, in his opinion.

But now Maya was back in India; she had left five years ago to the day, as a matter of fact. As Royce raised the tattered letter and began reading yet again, the emotions came flooding in, just as they had when he first read the words Maya had left for him upon her unexpected departure on that spring morning so long ago:

> *Royce,*
>
> *In one of our early conversations, I shared with you that I did not know what brought us together— and that was true. So many times in my life, I have wondered where I was being led and why, only to learn each time that I was exactly where I needed to be.*
>
> *Now, once again, this trust has been affirmed.*
>
> *I see clearly that the reason our lives intersected was to help heal you, to help heal me, and now, to empower you to use your gifts to heal the world.*
>
> *My enclosed copy of The Six Principles of Sacred Power is now yours. It explains and symbolizes the power you have finally discovered. Live out its lessons, and know you are free to pass this book and*

its message along as I did—and like me, you will know when the time is right to do so.

What you have learned so well is that we all have abilities that seem miraculous, yet these natural abilities have simply become hidden beneath layers of doubt, anxiety, and fear. Only when we are able to release these hindrances can we reveal the magnificent tools that have always been available to us. Sadly, most people are never able to do this—but with the carefully chosen sacred principles you have learned, hopefully you can change this. I believe you can . . . and will.

Likewise, I am so honored to share this sacred statue with you. It was given to my parents by Mr. Gandhi, who had commissioned it from a special sculptor in Madras. The piece represents my parents' pivotal work in Gandhi's movement. The star, of course, symbolizes India, as the two figures look to it for inspiration and dream of a brighter future for all citizens. Each time you look upon this gift, let the figures and their unified upward gaze remind you of the common work we are doing—although from different sides of the world.

You are a new man now, Royce. You understand that your ability to perform what some would call "miracles" is only limited by the power of your own belief. Your daughters, your friends, and anyone you meet will sense this difference in you and feel the spirit of unlimited belief you now possess—and it will bless their lives.

You have your work to do, and I have mine. But someday, I know our paths will cross again. Until then, I wish you Godspeed and great things on your journey.
Namaste,
Maya

As he looked up from the letter and stared once more out the window, Royce saw that the rain was finally beginning to taper off, as the evening darkness slowly, gently spread across the vast, wooded acreage. Pondering those times with Maya and everything that had transpired over the past five years, he reflected on his lingering despondency. Maybe it was time for a road trip, to help him regroup and recharge the old batteries. It had been a while since he had gotten away, and traveling was always therapeutic for him.

Yes, he thought, *a relaxing little vacation might be just what the doctor ordered.*

Royce stood up and headed to his bedroom to turn in a little early, still thinking about the past five years of his "new normal." His daughters, Becky and Emma, were now both in college. He had just written his ninth inspirational book. And as he stopped by the bathroom to brush his teeth, he looked in the mirror, then shook his head and smiled, remembering yet another birthday was just around the corner.

"Ah, yes . . . another day, a little more gray," he said with a laugh, running his fingers through his salt-and-pepper hair.

One thing was certain: Royce had lived his life differently since he met Maya all those years ago. The spiritual gifts she had shared through *The Six Principles of Sacred Power* only seemed to grow stronger and stronger within him. How would he ever have made it had he not met her? Now he was living in a way that was peaceful, powerful, and compassionate at a level he could never have dreamed. And as he lived out the principles, he found—just as Maya had said—that not only was *he* changed, but the people around him were changing, too.

Those who spent any length of time with Royce all seemed to say the same kinds of things: "I don't know why I feel so comfortable around you."; "I just feel like you don't judge me."; or even "Royce, I can't explain it, but you seem to give me the strength to be a better person!" No matter what their individual experience, they always expressed a sense of gratitude just for being with him. It was not only indescribably beautiful, but it was also downright surreal . . . and he was incredibly grateful, too.

Of course, he never shared anything about *The Six Principles of Sacred Power* with anyone, as much as he often wanted to do so. In fact, there were times he desperately wanted nothing more than to have *someone* with whom to share the whole experience.

Royce's daughters did not know about the principles either. They just knew their father was *different* after they returned from summer camp that memorable week five years ago . . . different in a very good way. Whatever had happened while they were away had been something wonderful—for all of them.

Back when Royce lost his wife in the accident, his daughters had been deeply concerned that their father would break under the stress and grief of it all. They watched him struggle with the immense sadness and discouragement—and even though they could empathetically relate, they knew that their father ultimately had to fight this battle on his own.

Yet incredibly, despite it all, Royce *didn't* break.

In fact, after his life-changing week with Maya, not only did he not break, but his girls watched the man in him rising to new heights of courage and strength—a man who would not only be able to take care of his family, but who now seemed miraculously capable of helping to heal the whole world.

But now, Royce had the distinct feeling there was *something more* waiting for him. As he thought back on his days as a young tennis professional, he remembered how he would achieve a new level of proficiency, then immediately want to push himself to the next level, striving to reach his full athletic potential. Now, he felt just the same about his spiritual potential.

In fact, he had a strange sense that he was somehow *destined* to fulfill this potential.

The question was . . . *how?*

If "Coach" Maya, as he so fondly called her, were here, she would surely give him the guidance and encouragement he needed. Alas, that was not possible.

So, Royce simply decided it was time for a short sabbatical. He would regroup, revitalize himself, and maybe get some clarity on how he could incorporate *The Six Principles of Sacred Power* into his life at this new level he felt was waiting for him. After all, he *was* tired. Certainly, he was exhilarated by all the change in his life and the amazing skills he had learned from the book. At the same time, he felt pulled in so many different directions that his strength was waning. Maybe a respite would take him back to the emotional and spiritual elevation he had reached through working with the book—and beyond.

Nodding in approval of his retreat decision, Royce smiled as he picked up his glass of water on the bathroom counter, savored the last few sips, and began eagerly thinking of the days ahead.

One of Royce's favorite getaway spots was a small island off the coast of southern Georgia, Jekyll Island. He had been born on the nearby atoll of St. Simons, just over the causeway, but his family had moved away when he was only a few years old. Still, there was something about the so-called Golden Isles that always seemed to call him back, so he visited the area regularly with his wife and children, discovering a variety of delightful new places each time. Then he had stumbled upon Jekyll Island, and the entire Holloway family immediately fell in love with it.

When they first visited, Jekyll was a quiet little place, not being particularly popular yet with the high-dollar vacationers from Atlanta. "Too rural and underdeveloped," such demanding tourists would say. But years later, the state of Georgia launched a plan to change all that—slowly, methodically, and beautifully. By the time the public began embracing the transformation that would make Jekyll Island a sought-after vacation spot, Royce and his family were already regulars . . . especially at the Jekyll Island Club Hotel.

A former winter home for such notable early-twentieth-century millionaire family names as Rockefeller, Goodyear, and Morgan, the Jekyll Island Club Hotel had the appearance of a huge Victorian mansion. Nowadays, it was gradually reclaiming its former reputation as a mecca of tranquility and beauty—one that travelers came from all over the world to visit. As the island was being redeveloped, the Jekyll Island Authority was taking special care to make the historic hotel the crown jewel of it all.

Yes—this was where Royce would go for his escape. Even a short time on the island would be perfect. With that decision made, he went ahead and quickly packed a bag with a few days' worth of essentials—including

The Six Principles of Sacred Power, of course. Checking the weather for the coast, he saw nothing out of the ordinary: warm, humid days with afternoon showers. *Typical Georgia summer weather,* he thought. The forecast did show a weakened hurricane limping up the east coast of Florida, but the report said it was on its last leg and headed out to sea, safely away from Jekyll Island. Double-checking the radar on another weather channel, he saw that the storm did indeed appear to be moving off to the east, putting his mind at ease. He mentally filed the information away and hopped into bed to do a little reading. In a short time, he was fully engaged in one of his favorite books on the unique history of Jekyll Island—which only increased his feeling of excitement about the upcoming trip.

After about thirty minutes, Royce put the book aside and reached into the top drawer of his nightstand and pulled out a folded, frayed piece of paper. He carefully unfolded it, then read the faded words aloud:

The Six Principles of Sacred Power

- *The Principle of Supreme Gentleness*
- *The Principle of Precision*
- *The Principle of Unshakable Generosity*
- *The Principle of Unending Appreciation*
- *The Principle of Inspirational Words*
- *The Principle of Unrelenting Persistence*

He never tired of reading these principles. After all, they had been a miraculous lifesaver for him during a horrible time of distress. Five years ago, as Maya shared the depth of the principles each day, he had felt himself becoming stronger, wiser, and more capable . . . until he finally reached a point where he sensed he could do *anything* he set his mind to. It was as if his true God-given abilities and faith had at long last suddenly been unleashed—and his world would never be the same.

Royce smiled, folded the paper back up, returned it to the drawer in his nightstand . . . and fell asleep as soon as his head hit the pillow.

CHAPTER 2

After a good night's rest, Royce awoke, put the coffee on, and jumped in the shower. As he felt the warm water cascade over his body, his mind wandered to the upcoming trip that day. Though the drive was nearly six hours long, he relished the journey to the coast, passing through the gentle rolling hills of central Georgia, on to the flat southern plains, then finally through the historical marshes of Glynn County, home to Jekyll Island. He was more than ready; he got the sense that this might just be one of his most memorable trips ever.

When he finally got in the car and began heading south, Royce slowly began to feel a sense of freedom. As he gazed out at the bright Southern sunshine, his mind involuntarily began to drift back to those days in the gardens with Maya. He wondered how she was doing in the powerful political position she had been appointed to in northern India—the position which led her away from the U.S. five years ago. He had thought of calling her periodically, but for some reason he never followed through, although they did occasionally exchange letters. Maya had always said she favored writing letters over making phone calls, even if they were "old-fashioned." She felt that words on paper created a unique tactile and emotional experience for both the writer and the recipient—and he'd realized as he corresponded with her that she was right. Of course, as an author, he loved writing and receiving letters, so that was perfect for him.

But after the first year, when they had established that Maya's work in India seemed to be on track and Royce's mission was equally on track, the letters dropped off. In fact, it had been almost two years since he had connected with her at all. However, he had no doubt she was changing the country. Every once in a while, he would read *The Times of India* and see her name written with great reverence. He wondered how many lives had been impacted by Maya's compassion, courage, and wisdom—and whether people knew just how fortunate they were to have such a special leader.

He further wondered if Maya ever thought about *him*. He supposed she must feel the same way every mentor feels about their prize students: wishing them well, and trusting they will use their gifts to improve the world in their own distinctive way. Of course, Royce knew *The Six Principles of Sacred Power* that Maya shared with him made him different from most pupils . . . not necessarily *better*, but the stakes and the expectations for him were now extraordinarily high. And even after all these years since their daily conversations in the Georgia countryside, he still did not want to let her down—ever.

Royce's mind came back to his present journey, and he watched the miles ticking off on the odometer. Passing through town after small country town, he finally reached the coastal area he had been eagerly envisioning since yesterday. He slowly let down his window as he approached the massive steel suspension bridge stretching from the mainland town of Brunswick over to Jekyll Island, feeling the moist coastal air blowing gently on his face. It never changed; every time he returned to the Golden Isles, it felt as if he were coming home—even though it had been almost fifty years since he lived on St. Simons Island. Crossing the towering bridge, Royce thought back on the countless times he had made this same crossing. He savored the memories of the many adventures he and his family had shared here, and the way that every time he arrived, the gigantic live oak trees of Jekyll Island seemed to invite him onto the massive grounds of the hotel, reaching out to welcome him, their trailing Spanish moss lazily swaying like gigantic, wispy gray beards in the soft Southern breeze.

Royce was finally back, and he felt like the luckiest man in the entire state of Georgia . . . at least for now.

CHAPTER 3

When Royce checked in, it was four in the afternoon. He headed up a flight of stairs to his traditional room—2218—dropped his bag on the floor, then stepped out onto the balcony to view the beautiful Jekyll Island shoreline. It was just as he remembered: the sailboats in the bay, the occasional dolphin diving through the shimmering water, the happy people strolling around the property. While it was a little disappointing that the clouds seemed to be rolling in, he assumed it was just the usual late afternoon showers approaching. He decided he would head back downstairs to go out for a walk before the burst of summer rain came through and steamed up the grounds in its aftermath. As he reached the bottom of the winding Victorian staircase, he turned to head out the side exit leading to the hotel's pristinely manicured gardens. But just as he opened the large double doors, the first raindrops began to fall, and he realized his afternoon survey of the grounds would have to wait.

Oh well, he thought, *guess I could make a quick stop at the bar . . .* Turning to his left, Royce took in the spectacular darkly stained bar and the lone person seated there, watching the large TV. *Maybe I can make a new friend and wait it out. A late afternoon cup of coffee might be a good way to wind down from the drive anyway.*

Royce plopped down a couple of seats away and saw that the man—likely in his late seventies or early eighties—was engrossed in watching a golf tournament while sipping his tea. Ordering a cup of coffee, Royce sat quietly, reflecting on the day's drive.

Suddenly, the older man came to life, exclaiming, "Now THAT'S a shot!"

Royce glanced up just in time to see the replay of a magnificent twenty-foot putt, which won the tournament for the excited youthful golfer.

"They're getting younger and younger," Royce piped up. "Or else, *we're* getting . . . well, you know."

The gentleman laughed in approval. Smiling, he reached his hand over the vacant seats toward Royce. "I'm Godfrey. Godfrey Tillman."

Royce smiled back, shaking the extended hand. "I'm Royce Holloway. Nice to meet you."

Strangely, when Godfrey looked at him, Royce got the uncanny sense that the man somehow already knew who he was. Plus, the name . . . Royce felt like he had heard it before.

But that wasn't possible . . . was it?

Royce immediately noticed that the stocky man had an air of tranquility and impeccability. His full gray hair was neatly cut and parted on the right side, his shirt was tailored, his soft brown shoes were shined, and his light blue jacket was tailored to perfection. He also had a subtle accent; Royce surmised that it was British.

"Where's home?" Royce asked.

The gentleman laughed loudly. "I've been trying to figure that out for a long time. I guess it's wherever I make it."

Royce paused, startled. He'd heard that very comment before . . . from Maya, the first day they met. Smiling, he mentally filed it away.

With a grin, Godfrey added, "Technically, I still claim to be from the UK . . . although most of my life, I've been a citizen of the world, I guess you could say."

A fellow traveler, then. Some of Royce's favorite conversations over the course of his life had been with folks who spent a great deal of time on the road, as he did. He laughed. "Yes, I feel that same way sometimes."

"So where are *you* from?" the gentleman urged.

"I was born here in the Golden Isles, but I've spent most of my life upstate, near Atlanta. I still come down here several times a year just to get back to my roots— and get some good seafood." Royce smiled.

"Well," the man countered with a grin, "it's not the fish and chips I'm used to, but it'll do."

The two travelers laughed heartily, and the conversation began flowing easily. Before he knew it, Royce had been talking with Godfrey for almost two hours—and as evening approached, the now steady rain had started coming down even heavier, much to his surprise and dismay.

Suddenly, a loud clap of thunder resounded through the bar—and it sounded close. But Godfrey did not even flinch as he serenely sipped his tea.

"Hmmm," Royce mused. "Sounds a little worse than the typical thundershowers."

"Agreed," Godfrey said. "But we'll be ok. These things do pass through fairly fast—even the intense ones, from what I hear."

Overhearing the conversation, the bartender, who up to that point had been quite aloof, decided to chime in. "That's typically true. But the weather conditions have continued to deteriorate over the last few hours, and it seems like this storm could be much worse than usual. On TV a little while ago, they were saying the hurricane may now actually strengthen, then turn and head back our way. I've never heard of a hurricane making that kind of shift, so hopefully they're wrong . . . but around here, you never know what might happen. The weather can change in no time."

Royce and Godfrey nodded somberly at the bartender's assessment, then resumed their conversation.

At one point, Royce asked, "Are you traveling alone?"

Godfrey paused, looking away, then slowly turned back to Royce. "Pretty much always have. Not many women are willing to put up with my constant travels—or with me, for that matter. Well, save for one. . ." Godfrey managed a slight smile as his voice trailed off.

With only a couple hours of conversation between them, Royce surprisingly felt comfortable enough with Godfrey to ask, "Feel like talking about it?"

Godfrey seemed to be debating whether or not he *did* want to talk about it, but then he slowly said, "It's a long story, as far as my earlier days with a companion go. But as for this trip, well. . ."

Royce braced himself, sensing that Godfrey was about to share something significant. He did not want to miss a word.

"Royce, I have a terminal blood disease. It's quite rare. Turns out the symptoms are often easy to miss, which was true in my case. I am in the final stage."

Royce was dumbfounded. He sat in silence as the older man continued.

"My doctor broke the news to me a few months ago. He suggested I take a nice, long vacation, to rest up before some of the treatments we were going to try." He smiled. "I agreed with him about the trip—I mean, I don't need many reasons to travel—but I didn't agree with him on the treatments. I just decided I would let the chips fall where they may, as you say here in America."

"Godfrey, I'm . . . so sorry," Royce stammered.

Godfrey shook his head and smiled. "Ah, my friend, all is well. My life has been nothing short of spectacular, and I'm grateful for every moment. Plus, I have now had the pleasure of traveling for the last three months, and the places I have been and the people I was able to see were worth every second."

Royce was intrigued. "Where all have you been over that time?"

"I decided I wanted to spend time with some of my wisest and dearest friends, as well as see some new places. So I bought an open-ended round-the-world ticket and left home ninety days ago. I have been to Morocco, then Switzerland, then Greece, India, China, Hawaii, and now. . ." He spread his arms appreciatively. ". . . the Golden Isles."

"And where will it end, Godfrey? Where is your last stop?"

"Well, that's the Lord's decision," he replied with a hearty laugh.

"No, no!" Royce managed to smile back, embarrassed by the inconsiderate phrasing of his question. "What I meant was, where is the last stop on your tour?"

"Ah, gotcha," said Godfrey with a wink. "That would be the island of Antigua."

"The eastern Caribbean! I've heard lots about it from a friend who's been there," added Royce. "Antigua is supposedly stunning, and it's definitely on my bucket list."

"Who knows . . . maybe you'll get to see it sooner rather than later," Godfrey replied with a mischievous grin.

Royce paused at the odd comment. But before he could ask the gentleman what he meant, Godfrey added, "Yes, it is stunning. I have lived for years in St. Paul parish, not too far from Nelson's Dockyard National Park, and I can't wait to get back. My flight is scheduled to leave tomorrow morning—if our Georgia weather cooperates, of course."

Royce nodded. "That's a big 'if,' I'm afraid."

As Godfrey started to respond, the door to the grounds suddenly burst open. A hotel employee rushed in with a frightened look on his face, his clothes sopping wet. "It's really getting bad out there. Who would have imagined. . . ? They're saying the hurricane has now completely changed direction from the forecast models, and it's picking up speed and heading right toward Jekyll Island! We're talking potentially hundred-mile-an-hour winds and ten inches of rain! I have never seen anything like this—it's apparently known as *rapid intensification*, and it caught even the weather forecasters off guard."

Godfrey just looked at the man and said quietly, "Looks like we may be in for a long night, my good man."

The ease and confidence with which he spoke gave Royce a surprising and much-needed boost of reassurance. He was thinking back to a hurricane he had weathered as a college student in Pensacola, Florida.

He'd had no previous experience with the destructive potential of such fierce storms, but after Category-4 Hurricane Frederic, he had told himself he would never go through anything like that again.

As Royce pondered his current predicament, Godfrey calmly reached over to grab a handful of peanuts out of the small glass bowl on the bar. It was then that Royce noticed the beautiful silver ring on Godfrey's right hand, bearing an impressive bright red stone.

"Your ring is spectacular. Rubies are my favorite stones," he said.

"Why, thank you. The ring is special to me," Godfrey responded with a smile. "It was given to me by a group of friends whom I spent a great deal of time with in India years ago." He took the ring off and handed it to Royce.

Royce admired the exquisite design. As he turned the ring over, he noticed *6-5-4* engraved on the inside of the band. Rather than ask a probing question, he raised an eyebrow and hesitantly commented, "India . . . I have a friend there—a special friend."

Godfrey paused for several seconds. Then he quietly commented, "Yes . . . I know."

Royce suddenly felt the blood draining from his face—and his pallor didn't go unnoticed by Godfrey. However, the gentleman remained quiet, waiting for Royce to speak.

"What do you mean, 'I know'?" Royce asked incredulously.

Godfrey responded in an unwavering tone, "I know Maya, Royce. I know her well."

Royce felt his head spinning. It was the same feeling he'd had when he first met Maya in the gardens five years ago.

"You can't *possibly* know her. There are over a billion people in India. How could you know her? How . . . how did you know I was on Jekyll? How did we end up here together at all?" Even after all the lessons Maya had taught Royce about belief and possibility and the fact that "there are no coincidences in this world," this all seemed . . . well, unbelievable. But as with so many other synchronistic encounters in Royce's years since meeting Maya, he intuitively knew this connection was meant to be.

What Godfrey said next instantly affirmed Royce's suspicions. "As far as how I know Maya, trust me, Royce—I will share that with you in due time. And as for how I knew you'd be on Jekyll now, I didn't *know* you would be here . . . but I *felt* you would be." He paused. "Then again, my 'feelings' over the years have actually turned more into 'knowings'—so I guess I *did* know you would be here, in a sense," he said with a smile.

Royce nodded, and despite the confusion he was feeling, he managed to smile back. He understood what Godfrey meant, even though the comment would sound quite odd to anyone else. Royce's intuition had been at an extraordinarily high level ever since he learned the unique lessons in *The Six Principles of Sacred Power,* and he could sense that Godfrey might have the same capability, though he wasn't yet sure how the older man would have acquired it.

"I knew our paths would cross at some point," Godfrey went on. "Maya asked me to check on you and let you know she was thinking of you. She told me all about your time in the gardens, and how special you are to her. She also wanted to make sure you knew she was okay—in case you'd heard the news."

"The news? What do you mean? How is she?" Royce demanded, mind still reeling.

Godfrey's countenance became solemn. After several seconds, he replied, "She's fine . . . now." In response to Royce's panicked look, he continued, "Maya has been a very popular politician in northern India, as you can imagine . . . well, with most people. There were and are some extremists, however, whose radical views do not align with Maya's more conservative vision. Still, she always wants to be out with the people, and when she is in public, she walks beside her motorcade rather than riding in a protected vehicle, so she can look people in the eyes and shake their hands. Early one day last spring, Maya's motorcade was ambushed, and she was shot. The bullet hit about six inches from her heart, close to her shoulder. A gunfight ensued, and the four assailants were killed, as was one of Maya's bodyguards."

Royce couldn't believe it. This was his mentor—the kind, wise, mystical woman who had helped him so much. This woman had changed his life, empowering him with the faith that he could do things he had never believed possible. How could anyone do this to her?

"Godfrey, how is she doing now?" asked Royce, voice quivering.

"The village where the ambush took place did not have adequate medical facilities, so they rushed her to New Delhi, about an hour away. She was minutes from death, but they got her to the hospital just in time. The surgery lasted eight hours, and gratefully she pulled through and has now fully recovered."

"It's just unreal," Royce murmured as he buried his face in his hands.

Godfrey continued, "The press reported that when Maya was in the hospital and was finally able to stand, she walked to the window, parted the curtains, looked outside . . . and saw a crowd of over ten thousand people waving and cheering for her. It must have been incredible."

A broad smile came over Royce's face as he quietly said, "Doesn't surprise me at all."

"Agreed," said Godfrey. "Now Maya is more popular than ever. But as you know, she cares nothing about popularity. She simply cares about making a positive difference in India—and the world."

Royce nodded in agreement.

Just then, the bar phone rang. Upon answering, the bartender listened intently, then hung up and turned to Royce and Godfrey with a serious look on his face. "The winds have picked up even more. The hotel has issued a voluntary evacuation—but the manager strongly recommends that everyone should leave as soon as possible. There is a large storm shelter on the west side of the island, and all the guests and staff are heading there now. The manager is also preparing to leave . . . which means the three of us are about to be the only ones left in the hotel."

"Well, Godfrey, I guess we have no choice," Royce replied.

Godfrey shot back, "There's always a choice, my good man. And the biggest choice right now is whether my next cup will be Earl Grey or green tea."

"What?" Royce said in disbelief.

Godfrey laughed. "Well, I know it's odd for an Englishman to drink green tea, but I learned to like it quite a bit when I visited friends in Singapore. I—"

"Godfrey, are you serious?" Royce cut in. "They're telling us to get out of the hotel!"

"They are merely *suggesting* we vacate the premises," Godfrey corrected him. "I choose not to accept their kind offer."

"What do you mean? The storm is headed right for us, and we're about to be the only people left here!"

Godfrey's words were calm, yet firm. "Royce, I have been on this earth for eighty glorious years. If my time ends here at this beautiful place, I am blessed. If I make it back to Antigua, I am also blessed. I shall stay . . . yet you, of course, are free to go."

Royce just stared at Godfrey. He thought of Becky and Emma. Then he thought of his life up until this moment. He, too, had been blessed—and now this time with Godfrey felt more than just special; it seemed *sacred*. Also, he was sensing he had only uncovered the tip of the iceberg as far as this gentleman's incredible journey went.

But the storm. . . he reminded himself.

"Godfrey, I'm afraid I have made my choice," Royce said softly.

"I understand," Godfrey replied dispassionately.

"Yes, I think . . . I'll choose the green tea this time." Royce grinned.

Godfrey slapped his knee and leaned back, smiling broadly. "A fine choice, indeed. I think I'll do the same, my friend."

Right then, heavy rain began blowing loudly against the window. Within minutes, the bartender, having overheard their last bit of conversation, set their drinks in front of them and quickly put on his rain jacket. "Here's a full pot of green tea . . . and some candles and matches, which I hope you won't need. Unfortunately,

I must go. Good luck, gentlemen," the young man said coolly as he exited the bar.

At that moment, the old grandfather clock chimed eight times, and as the winds began to roar eerily outside, Royce realized he and Godfrey were now all alone in the Jekyll Island Club Hotel.

CHAPTER 4

As their conversation continued into the night, the storm, oddly enough, seemed to simply fade into the background—although the strength of the storm did not fade at all.

Royce walked over to the large window, which looked out on the hotel grounds. "There must be nearly six inches of rain out there," he muttered with a degree of concern.

"That's almost half a foot, if I calculate correctly," Godfrey cackled.

Royce shook his head and laughed, then returned to the bar.

"Let's move into the next room," Godfrey offered.

"Ah, the library! It's one of my favorite places in the hotel. Great idea," Royce responded with enthusiasm.

They settled in at a small table beside a row of four tall shelves full of hundreds of wonderful old books. Like everything else in the room, the bookshelves were constructed of mahogany in the classic Victorian style. Royce thought about the influential conversations that must have taken place over the last hundred years in this room. Surely many business tycoons, educators, inventors, and other great thinkers had visited the island in that time, and perhaps from this very library, they had launched ideas and projects that had impacted the world.

"Godfrey, may I ask you a question?" Royce said quietly.

Godfrey grinned. "I've got no place to go, as we have established."

Royce smiled back, but before he could speak, Godfrey's expression turned serious, and he said, "I assume there's a question of interest coming, not just one of curiosity." Then he couldn't help but slip back into a grin.

Royce laughed loudly, recalling that during their discussions, Maya had continually reminded him of the importance of asking spiritually expansive questions of genuine interest, as opposed to self-centered questions of mere curiosity. "Oh, believe me, I learned that lesson. It's definitely a question of interest," he said with a chuckle. Then he asked gently, "Your attitude. . . it's so inspiring to me, especially considering the burden you are carrying. How do you do it?"

Godfrey looked at Royce as a grandfather would look at his favorite young grandson. "Royce, burdens aren't burdens until we choose to label them that way. Each of us is dealt a hand in life that perhaps we wouldn't have chosen for ourselves. But as we get comfortable with the uncertainty of the cards we hold, we realize they are the exact ones we needed in order to learn the lessons we are destined to learn."

Royce nodded. "I understand; I have had my share of those cards. But don't you ever feel like complaining?"

"Feel like it? Certainly. Actually complain? No. Not only is it incredibly disempowering, but I also understand that everyone has their own challenges—so no one particularly wants to hear mine." Godfrey smiled. "My position is that every person has a choice: they can bear their burdens gracefully and use them to grow, help others, and make the world a better place . . . or they can just complain about them, and help no one. My motto is 'Nothing is a big deal, unless I choose to make it a big deal.' "

"So you *never* complain? You'll have to excuse me, but it all sounds rather stoic to me," Royce replied quizzically.

Godfrey shook his head. "Well, of course I slip up now and then—but I quickly catch myself. Maybe some people would see this as 'stoic' behavior, but I don't think of it that way. It is just the path I have chosen, and it works better for me. I used to be a complainer, when I was much younger . . . but later on, I realized that my griping had its roots in fear and lack of self-confidence. I needed other people's approval, so I justified my negative behavior and thoughts with complaints and pessimistic comments. Funny thing is, once I came to understand this, the less I complained—and the more confident and courageous I became."

Royce's thoughts were racing as he absorbed Godfrey's wise words. There were so many similarities between Maya and this gentleman in their poise, their attitude, and their philosophy of life. "Godfrey, how are you connected to Maya?" he finally asked.

At that moment, Godfrey coughed loudly and deeply. Royce suddenly realized that the older man had coughed this way at the bar several times before, and concern crossed his face at the unusual raspy sound of it.

Slightly embarrassed, Godfrey smiled matter-of-factly and simply offered, "The old cough is not getting a whole lot better, I guess." Then he moved on, his look growing distant as he reflected on the question. When he spoke, however, it was clearly and with authority. "Ah, yes, Maya . . . I suppose it would be useful if I shared the story of meeting her father, as that is how the connection began."

Royce leaned in, listening intently.

"You see, I owned a small shipping company in London when I was in my early thirties. The business was started by my own father, and then he passed it along to me as his health began declining in his later years. I was terrified; I didn't think I had the skill or the wisdom my father had, so I didn't know if I could succeed."

"Every son feels that way, I think," Royce chimed in. "Especially when we are trying to fill the shoes of great people."

"Well, my father was certainly a great man . . . which I guess is why I wanted to succeed so badly: to make him proud of me. I just couldn't let him down. The business indeed came close to failing soon after I took over, but I was determined. That's the word: 'determined.' Eventually, I got a hold on what I was doing, and the company started to prosper. Within five years, we had expanded to multiple locations around the world."

"Incredible," Royce murmured.

"Yes, it was an exciting time. Auckland, Hong Kong, Nairobi, Gibraltar, Madras. . . I still clearly remember them all. But Madras—that location was significant. It was where I met Livingston, Maya's father."

Having spent time in India during his younger days when he had played on the professional tennis tour, Royce's ears perked up. "Madras has some of the most beautiful coastal scenery in all of India."

"It *is* a beautiful place," replied Godfrey. "That day was wonderful . . . and also *not* so wonderful." At Royce's perplexed look, Godfrey continued. "As you know, during those years, England had an icy grip on India. However, I spent a lot of time in my company's Indian branch, since I loved the country so much. Sometimes I was there for months, and I even had a home in Madras. As I did business there, the Indian people were always kind to me; I assume it was because I loved my Indian employees and treated them like family. I'm sure it didn't hurt that I also paid them unusually well."

"Doesn't surprise me, Godfrey. From what I can tell so far, it's just the type of person you are. You see only *people*—not their age, ethnicity, nationality, or anything else," Royce offered.

"It's the way my parents raised me—and I guess I just continued following their lead," Godfrey nonchalantly replied. "So, one sunny afternoon, I was standing out back behind the office building in Madras, having a smoke. Our location there backed up to a British neighborhood, which was separated from our office by a fence, and of course, Indian locals were forbidden to be in that area. The bobbies patrolled the vicinity to make sure that rule was enforced. Well, out of the corner of my eye, I saw a small dog crawl under the fence and trot into the neighborhood. Then right behind the little dog, I saw an Indian girl, about ten years old, trying in vain to catch the animal before it got into the British zone. The girl wiggled underneath the fence and started running after the pup—but unfortunately, a rather large, unfriendly bobby saw and grabbed her right before she caught her dog."

Royce's anxious look indicated he knew what was coming next, but he sat still as Godfrey's narrative unfolded.

"He shoved the child with such force that it knocked her to the ground, and he began screaming at her in English, which of course she didn't understand. The girl started crying loudly, and that infuriated the bobby even more. As he slowly raised his truncheon to teach the girl a lesson, I couldn't bear to watch anymore. I dashed from my spot, leapt over the fence, and lay down over the child to shield her from the impending blow. As the hits began landing on my back, I felt I would pass out . . . but somehow, I managed to turn and grab the weapon while I still had my wits—and any strength left.

"Not only did I grab the club, I also grabbed the man's throat with my other hand. The terrified look on his face scared even me, knowing what I was doing, but anger and survival mode had taken over. I think I would have killed him . . . but suddenly, out of nowhere, a tall, strong man appeared and pulled me off him. It was Livingston—someone I had heard much about, but had never met in person. Somehow, he pulled me away in a manner that was almost effortless, in one quick movement—and I weighed almost two hundred pounds at that time. The aura about him was one that the bobby and I sensed immediately. It's difficult to describe, even today; Livingston's action was compassionate, but it was also done in a way that commanded respect from both of us. It may sound odd, but it was as if the bobby and I were both changed in that moment, from being adversaries to simply two human beings connected by Livingston's positive energy."

Royce nodded. He knew that the kind of immediate transformation Godfrey was describing would indeed have sounded strange to most people, but after reading *The Six Principles of Sacred Power*, he found it perfectly feasible.

Godfrey continued, "After that moment, the bobby actually picked the child up and handed her the dog, which had lovingly run back to her side. The man even walked the girl and the pup to the fence, boosted them up, and gently set them down on the other side to go back to their nearby home. He then opened the gate for Livingston and me to exit. . . The whole experience was simply astonishing."

Royce was captivated by the story, but a question occurred to him. "How in the world did Maya's father happen to be there at that exact moment? Either you, the bobby, or both could likely have been killed otherwise. What a stroke of luck!"

Godfrey looked at Royce with the same look Maya had often given him in the gardens years ago, when he would ask questions that seemed to show a lack of faith. "It was not luck at all, Royce," he said with a smile. "You and I don't think in terms of luck, chance, or coincidence. We know we live in the realm of divine timing and carefully orchestrated purpose. Everything happened that day *exactly* as it was supposed to happen."

Royce nodded. "Yes, the divine plan is another lesson Maya drilled into my head—but obviously, there are times I still forget. There truly is no place for 'luck' in the lives of people who are on the path to spiritual mastery. I stand corrected."

"Yes . . . and if things had not happened the way they did, I would likely never have met Maya's father, *or*

Mr. Gandhi—and I would certainly never have learned about *The Six Principles of Sacred Power.*"

A chill ran up Royce's spine. At that moment, it occurred to him that Godfrey Tillman must be one of the original six leaders under Mahatma Gandhi—and undoubtedly a very powerful, very spiritual man.

CHAPTER 5

In the late 1800s and early 1900s, the Jekyll Island Club Hotel had a reputation for attracting the most elite and successful people of the era. What is now the hotel was at that time simply the "clubhouse," and the ultra-affluent built homes around it, eventually creating an idyllic community where their families would spend their winters, leaving the cold weather back in places like Philadelphia, New York, and Boston.

But in the 1940s, during World War II, after more than half a magical century, the government forced an evacuation of the island's wealthy inhabitants, due to concerns that a German submarine might make its way across the Atlantic Ocean to the Georgia shoreline. If the Germans decided to attack the island, they could not only destroy Jekyll, but they could also endanger the financial system of the entire United States: the full roster of the island's inhabitants at that time controlled approximately twenty percent of the country's wealth. The mandated evacuation was so swift that many personal items were eerily left behind—furniture, photographs, even dinnerware in some cases, perfectly set for the next meal. Almost overnight, the island became a virtual coastal ghost town.

The departure of its residents precipitated the inevitable and unfortunate ending of a unique and magnificent chapter of Jekyll Island history, and the clubhouse and surrounding homes soon fell into disrepair. Eventually, the state of Georgia ended up purchasing the island and began slowly, painstakingly rebuilding the Jekyll Island clubhouse into a magnificent hotel, with the old houses around it also being restored to their former glory. Some homes came to serve as additional accommodations, while others were converted into buildings that supported the operations of the hotel. After ongoing renovations lasting almost thirty years, the hotel and its adjoining properties were brilliantly reborn for the masses to enjoy, fortuitously protected from most tropical storms and hurricanes thanks to the barrier islands that shielded it.

But not this time.

As the winds howled and the rain pelted the old hotel like a barrage of angry bullets, Royce had to wonder if the Jekyll Island Club Hotel and its two remaining inhabitants would make it through, not only unscathed, but make it through at all. Yet even with the impending, potentially devastating hurricane, after hearing Godfrey mention *The Six Principles of Sacred Power,* there was no storm on earth that could pull Royce away from his time with this special man.

"Godfrey—so you knew Mr. Gandhi, *and* you know about the Six Principles! But . . . how?"

Godfrey leaned back in his chair and took a deep breath. "After the incident with the security guard in Madras, Livingston invited me to meet a close friend of his whom he happened to be seeing that evening. That friend was Mahatma Gandhi."

Royce calmly nodded, as if the comment did not surprise him at all—because it didn't. "What was he like?" he wondered aloud.

"Just like you would think, I assume. He was a gentleman's gentleman. When Livingston took me to meet him that night, our gathering spot was a small cottage near the coast. It was dark outside, so no one could see our meeting; even the front porch had no light on. There was a small candle in the window, which had been lit by the owner of the home—a supporter of the movement—to help us recognize the correct house. We knocked on the door, and when we were let in, the room was dark . . . but there, silhouetted by the fire, was Mahatma Gandhi, peacefully sitting cross-legged on the floor. He turned to us, smiled, and quietly offered, 'Namaste, gentlemen.' "

Royce felt goosebumps arise at the thought of what that initial introduction must have felt like to Godfrey.

"When Livingston and I sat down in the den with Mr. Gandhi, it was totally surreal to me. Being in the presence of a man who had already had such an impact on the world was indescribable. But what he did next was a powerful example of authentic compassion that I will always remember: he began speaking to me *like a friend*—even though I was an Englishman. I suppose the fact that I had entered the home with Livingston gave me instant credibility.

" 'Livingston told me of your bravery today,' Gandhi said. 'Not only that, but I have also heard from many of your employees regarding your kindness to them. I am honored to meet you.' "

Godfrey paused. "*Mahatma Gandhi* was honored . . . to meet *me*. Right then, I realized I had already learned a lesson from this powerful yet gentle man: everyone, including me, wants to be valued and appreciated. It's a philosophy I have lived by ever since that moment."

Royce was taking in every word of Godfrey's narrative as the gentleman continued.

"I had always had empathy for the plight of the Indian people. Seeing many of my countrymen treat the Indians so poorly was something I abhorred. Yet the only way I felt like I could help was to provide for my employees, both financially and emotionally. Then that day with the bobby . . . when I saw what almost happened to that young girl . . . I knew something had to change. I knew *I* had to 'be the change' I wished to see in the world, as Mahatma famously instructed us."

Still in awe, Royce smiled and chimed in, "Livingston introducing you to Mr. Gandhi must have been one of the greatest days of your life."

"Well, that's true . . . but remember, that was the day I met Livingston as well. Quite honestly, his temperament and spirit were much like Gandhi's. Both were amazing men, and I wanted to be like them. More importantly, I wanted to be *with* them; I wanted to be on their side, making a difference to the Indian people.

"After a conversation that lasted late into the night at this covert location, I was asked by Mr. Gandhi to join his peaceful resistance, as one of his elite six leaders. I did not hesitate; it was a dream come true. I knew, however, that like Livingston, I was putting my life on the line, but I also knew I could never live with myself if I didn't take the opportunity."

Royce stared in disbelief. What were the odds of running into this man, on this small island, in this very hotel? He shook his head mutely.

Godfrey seemed to know precisely what the younger man was thinking. "It's not about odds, Royce. It's about the power of belief, as Maya taught you. It's about living in faith, so that life happens precisely as it is supposed to happen, making the world a better place for us all."

"I see you have the same little gift that Maya has of tuning into others' thoughts," Royce said with a grin.

Godfrey smiled. "The same gift that you have now, if I am not mistaken, Royce. In fact, it is an example of the abilities that are available to us all—if we only *believe* that God has given them to us."

"Of course, Godfrey. I know now for certain you are correct." Royce pressed on. He had so many questions, just as he had during his time with Maya years ago. He was a man thirsting for knowledge—and his thirst could not be quenched quickly enough. "Speaking of gifts, I understood from Maya that the members of the original group under Mr. Gandhi—all six of you—each had different spiritual gifts that enhanced the power of the group. What was yours?"

Godfrey looked up as he leaned back in his chair, locked his hands behind his head, and paused in thought.

". . . Generosity."

As Royce listened closely, Godfrey continued. "With my business, I had the resources to help fund the movement, which I was honored to do. I guess you could call it a form of what the Indians referred to as *swadeshi*, or economic noncooperation against the British government, since it kept a lot of money in India to benefit the Indian people. Of course, very few people knew that it was me who provided the necessary amount of rupees for our operations."

Royce cut in. "It must have been in the millions, Godfrey. You are very humble."

Godfrey shook his head. "Again, it was simply an honor. I have always believed—and still do—that there will forever be more money available. So I never hoarded it, or any other resources. I just put the funds where I knew they would help the most people, and I let the good Lord take care of it—and take care of me—from there. Worked out okay, I guess." Godfrey grinned.

"I would say so," Royce said with a smile. Although he was a successful author, he had never met someone with resources like Godfrey Tillman possessed. "Godfrey, may I ask what it's like to earn *that* kind of money?"

Godfrey shrugged his shoulders. "Making money is relatively easy. The hard part—and the part people seem to avoid—is mastering the three steps leading up to making money. First, it's coming up with an idea that will work—which takes time and great focus. Second, it's *starting* the project or business. Most people can come up with a viable idea, but they do not act on it. Finally, once one begins, the third step is simply sticking with it until you see the idea to fruition. 'Unrelenting persistence,' as *The Six Principles of Sacred Power* calls it." He smiled again.

" 'Unrelenting persistence.' I have seen the power of that principle play out in my life again and again, ever since Maya taught me," Royce responded.

Godfrey nodded. "It is powerful—and so is generosity itself. I never cease to be amazed by the results of unselfish, trusting magnanimity . . . even down to the smallest act."

"I guess the more we give, the more that comes back to us, right?"

"Maybe," Godfrey replied neutrally.

Royce raised a quizzical eyebrow. "What do you mean?"

Godfrey hesitated for a moment, then thoughtfully replied, "Some people think that there's a kind of karmic accounting system in place—and who knows; maybe there is. However, I believe when we do things with the expectation of seeing a return, then our expectations become distorted, and our motive for doing the right and generous thing becomes more like an act of selfishness."

"Ah, yes, that makes sense," Royce agreed. He smiled, then his questioning mind shifted gears. "Speaking of karmic accounting . . . so the British never knew that one of their own was supplying funds for the peaceful revolution?"

Godfrey laughed. "No, they didn't have any idea—but I will say that definitely took some *creative* accounting. They tried to trace the money many times, but thankfully, they were never able to do so," he commented with pride. "However, that also meant I had to stay well under the radar. After the revolution ended, I retreated into relative anonymity; only Mahatma, Livingston, and Maya knew where I was, and they all swore never to divulge this. I only participated in one of the leadership group's reunions, and I have lived quietly on Antigua for many years. It's just much simpler—and there are still people out there, believe it or not, who are trying to piece together theories of my connection with Mr. Gandhi's team."

"But now you're traveling the world openly. . . ?"

"Well, Royce, it's my last hurrah, so to speak. At this point, I want to make sure I leave no unfinished business. I want to spend time with the people that have made my life so rich, and with their families. Most of the people I have visited on my farewell tour are the heirs of Mahatma's original team. Like you, these men and women are of course endowed with special abilities from reading *The Six Principles of Sacred Power*, which was typically passed on to them by a parent. My time with them has been incredible over the last few months, and it is clear they are truly changing our world for the better."

"The more I practice the Six Principles and see the results of my actions, the more I understand how critical our role is in making a difference in the lives of others—and the world," Royce offered.

When Godfrey heard these words, for the first time since they had sat down and begun their conversation hours before, he suddenly had a look of what seemed to be sadness. He stared pensively into the distance for what felt like several minutes, until his voice unsteadily broke the silence in the room. "There's more truth to that than you may know, Royce. Let me explain. . ."

CHAPTER 6

Royce wondered if he had said something to hurt Godfrey's feelings; that was the last thing he wanted to do. "Godfrey . . . I, um, didn't mean to. . ."

Godfrey raised his hand to stop Royce and softly replied, "Not at all, my friend. There are some lessons in life that are much harder than others—but still, they must be learned. For some reason, your comment reminded me of a lesson I am still trying to recover from *not* learning soon enough."

Royce looked puzzled.

"I said earlier that I would tell you about my former traveling partner," Godfrey went on. "Or shall I say . . . my former wife."

Royce tried to hide his surprise. He nodded tentatively, encouraging Godfrey to continue his story at whatever pace he chose.

"I met her when we were both nineteen, at the University of London. She was . . . a gorgeous woman. We fell in love so quickly, although I am not sure what she saw in me," he said with a hint of a smile. "I was awkward and shy, and she was like a princess—so graceful and charming. Our years in school flew by, and soon after, we were married. We both came from well-heeled families, so our early years of marriage were not typical, I guess you would say. We traveled to places like Paris, Rome, and Madrid, went to fine restaurants, met wonderful people . . . it was a fairy-tale existence.

". . . Or so I thought. What I *didn't* realize at the time was that even though she did not have to work outside the home, I worked *too* much—much too much. She tried to tell me she needed more of me, yet I felt so compelled to make my mark with the family business, I came home exhausted every night. I guess I made less and less time for her, and I spent more and more time focusing on my own worries and stressors with the business. I was too blind to see. . ."

"I understand," Royce replied empathetically. "It happens so easily."

"Yes, far too easily," agreed Godfrey. "Then one day, I came home to find a note that said she was destined to live her life somewhere else—somewhere she would feel cared for and loved." Tears rolled down his weathered cheeks as he went on, "It has been many years since she left, but I've scarcely gotten over it. We had no children, and when I lost her, I felt as if I was all alone—and at times, I still feel that way."

"It's ironic, isn't it?" Royce softly replied, his tone poignant and philosophical. "As men, we feel like we are doing the noble thing, working hard and providing for our family, especially when we are young—climbing the ladder to success. Then we often reach a point where we look down and see that we have been climbing to the wrong destination."

Godfrey dried his eyes and then rubbed his chin, pondering Royce's statement. "You may be right. However, even though it obviously still saddens me to think of how different things could have been, I do believe 'wrong' is a relative term. In my case, had things not gone the way they did, I would never have gotten to meet Mr. Gandhi, Livingston, or all the wonderful people in the movement . . . or you."

Royce smiled in appreciation, then offered, "Speaking of 'meet' . . . how about we see if we can scrape up a little meat, or something else to eat? I'm starving."

"Jolly good idea, mate," Godfrey said as he managed a smile. "Let's see what our friends at the hotel have on hand in the kitchen. We'll certainly leave them a few dollars in return for their kindness."

The pair left the library and headed down the hall into the hotel dining room, then made their way through a set of double doors into the kitchen, with the mischievous air of two giddy schoolboys sneaking into a deserted cafeteria. Opening one of the huge pantries, Royce reached for a large bag of potato chips, upon which Godfrey quipped, "I see you have shifted genres, from self-help to 'help yourself.' "

"Clever, Godfrey." Royce smiled. "I do feel like I am quickly moving from 'best-selling author' to 'best-stealing author.' "

Godfrey laughed heartily as the two men gathered their goodies—chips, cheese, nuts, and a few bottles of water—left a fifty-dollar bill and a note of thanks, then headed back to the main lounge area by the bar.

The wind had picked up tremendously as they settled in for more conversation.

"It's got to be blowing at least fifty miles an hour," remarked Royce.

"Undoubtedly," replied Godfrey. "Could become unnerving for lesser men, don't you think?" He grinned.

"No doubt about it," Royce shot back with a laugh.

"When a man is put in a situation where he may not live to share that experience with anyone, it changes him . . . sometimes for the best, I might add. Tell me, Royce, have you ever been in a situation where you feared you wouldn't survive?"

Godfrey's question caught Royce off guard. He thought for a moment, took a sip of water, then replied, "I suppose the time that most easily comes to mind would be my honeymoon."

Godfrey had to laugh. "Good grief, old chap, she must have been quite dissatisfied to have threatened you to that extent!"

"No, no," Royce responded with a chuckle, then launched into the story. "It was a summer evening, and my new wife and I were both in our twenties. Our wedding had been held only hours before, on a little farm in Georgia, under a bright blue sky and a gorgeous setting Southern sun. We were ecstatic. Thinking of our new life together, we left the reception and headed to the airport to depart for our honeymoon in New England, wondering what adventures we would find there. Little did we know. . ."

Godfrey raised a curious eyebrow, wondering where the story would lead.

"On our flight from Atlanta, we were preparing for the descent into Boston. The night was clear, and there was a stunning, full moon over the city. But for some reason, the plane did not descend toward the airport. It turned away and began circling widely, apparently in a holding pattern. An hour later, as we completed our fourth circle over the city, the pilot's voice came over the intercom with the dreaded news: 'Ladies and gentlemen, it appears that our landing gear will not extend. We are running out of fuel, so we will attempt a landing without the gear in its proper position.' "

Godfrey was mesmerized as Royce continued.

"In a few moments, the captain's solemn voice again crackled across the PA system. He warned us that we would see emergency vehicles awaiting our landing, 'just in case'—then gave us the dire directive to 'prepare for impact.' "

Royce seemed to be reliving those horrible moments as his voice quivered and the pace of his words slowed. "The plane began its approach. As we braced for impact, my mind was consumed with the awful irony of the situation. *Incredible*, I thought. *This is how it all ends—when I believed our life together was just getting started.* . . I looked at my new bride, and seeing the tears in her eyes only affirmed that this would likely be the last time I would ever see her. I wiped the tears away, told her I loved her, and then we just waited. . ."

Godfrey nodded grimly as Royce's story came to its conclusion.

"Suddenly, without warning, the landing gear clunkily dropped into position—only seconds before the plane would have hit the ground, in an undoubtedly tragic way. As the wheels screeched across the runway and the plane came safely to a halt, my wife and I, and all the other passengers, were abruptly aware of the outcome that only moments ago had seemed unthinkable: *we had survived*. As we cautiously looked out the window, we saw the runway lined with a parade of ambulances, fire trucks, police cars, and other emergency vehicles in preparation for the impending disaster, just as the pilot had said. All my wife and I could do was hold each other and weep. . ."

The look on Godfrey's face was a combination of shock and relief. "My good man, I cannot fathom the terror you must have felt. It was a horrible circumstance indeed. To be in a situation like that is something I am sure few people understand."

"Yes," agreed Royce. "But in retrospect, there was an inherent gift in that scenario."

"Do tell, Royce," Godfrey urged.

"My happiness is one hundred percent up to me—but I needed a wake-up call to remind me that I am in control of it. That control can't be taken away. What *can* be taken away is the time I have left to act on that knowledge . . . so I have tried to keep that precious opportunity in mind each day."

"Bravo," Godfrey applauded. "Truly, that is the holy grail: understanding that each of us can choose happiness at any moment in our lives. Sadly, most people ignore this until a tragedy—or a potential tragedy—befalls them. They don't appreciate the multitude of gifts available to them in their lives . . . until they are looking into the eyes of something that can take it all away."

"Right," agreed Royce. "That had been true for me most of my life—even at times after I experienced that near-death event. However, once I fully understood the connected pieces of *The Six Principles of Sacred Power,* I knew that I would always have an irretractable sense of gratitude within me. To this day, the more grateful

I am, the more of the world's goodness and beauty I seem to find."

Godfrey nodded his approval. Just as he started to respond, their focus was shattered by a large metal JEKYLL ISLAND sign flying past the window and slamming into the building with a thunderous crash.

Royce was badly shaken. He thought he heard Godfrey ask him a question, but he couldn't process anything but fear. The potentially lethal sign hurtling through the air had brought back traumatic memories of the powerful hurricane he'd survived so many years ago, and he cringed when he thought of how fortunate he had been to survive that one.

As much as he didn't want to admit it, Royce was realizing that this time, he might not be so lucky.

CHAPTER 7

As Royce continued to reflect, his thoughts were now fully on the hurricane he had gone through in Pensacola. College had been thirty years ago, and sometimes it seemed to him as if he had forgotten nearly all of what he'd learned in his academic classes. But he had never forgotten Hurricane Frederic; every single moment was forever etched into his brain.

Anyone who has been through a monster coastal storm and was blessed to survive it has a similar "etching" in their brain. They are intimately familiar with the chill that runs up one's spine simply from hearing the word *hurricane*. All storms can be frightening, but there is something about a hurricane that puts it in a class by itself. Perhaps it's the duration of the storm; they can last for hours, and every hour feels like a godforsaken day. Menacing black clouds pour out a seemingly endless deluge of rain that stings like needles for anyone foolish enough to step outside. Beyond that, the bellowing winds can quickly become capable of lifting and catapulting that same unwary person for blocks, or even miles. Then, just when everything becomes uncannily quiet and it appears that the storm has vanished like a thief in the night, one has the horrific realization that it is simply the calm before the next round of destruction. Only then does one fully understand the concept of "the eye of the storm." The back side of the ghastly tempest now moves in, with the wind whipping from the opposite direction. The flooding continues—and at this point, it is even more likely that tornadoes will be spawned, unleashing an additional fury of nature upon the storm's helpless victims.

When the punishment eventually ends and a fortunate survivor is finally able to emerge from their sheltering place, the hurricane has left its calling card in the form of horrors such as huge road signs twisted up like pieces of flimsy foil, boats plunged into houses, and various large objects embedded like missiles in walls and roofs, angrily impaling targets previously believed to be impenetrable.

Royce remembered sitting in his apartment with a group of college buddies during the storm, occasionally—and foolishly—walking over to the window and watching the tall, sturdy palm trees continuously bending until their tops nearly touched the saturated ground. He remembered the "hurricane party," which had *seemed* like a great idea at the time. It numbed the fear for a short while . . . until one of the partygoers turned on the radio, broadcasting the grim reality of their situation as the tearful reporter announced that Mobile, Alabama, where the hurricane had made landfall—only a short distance away—was now "in ruins."

Miraculously, the apartment complex received only minor damage and the group made it through that night unharmed. But when they walked outside the next morning, the surrounding area could only be likened to a disaster-stricken war zone in a devastated third-world country. . .

Royce's thoughts shifted back to his current dilemma. He couldn't help but question his decision to stay at the hotel with Godfrey. But then again, something told him this was *exactly* where he was supposed to be—and since his days with Maya, Royce was not one to question "the still, small voice" inside.

Abruptly, Godfrey's booming British voice broke through Royce's wandering train of thought. "Royce, did I lose you, my good fellow?" he asked, playfully shaking the younger man's shoulder.

Royce sheepishly looked at Godfrey and apologized for his errant attention. "Sorry about that, Godfrey. I just . . . well, kind of went down memory lane for a moment."

Godfrey chuckled. "I understand. I find myself strolling down that lane all too often. And speaking of going places, I want to share the full reason I ended up at this place with you, Royce . . . or maybe I should say, the reason I was *led* to be here with you."

"The reason you were *led* here?" Royce asked with a perplexed look.

Godfrey nodded and then said, "First, let me ask you something, Royce: how have the Six Principles changed you over the last five years?"

Royce shook his head and answered, "I almost don't know where to start; my life has become different on many levels. I had so much anxiety and self-doubt before, but now, if I truly desire to accomplish something, my first thought is a confident 'Yes, that's possible, try it,' instead of 'Why would you even consider that?' "

Godfrey nodded. "Excellent. What else?"

"The traits in *The Six Principles of Sacred Power* have become ingrained in me," Royce continued thoughtfully. "I have developed a spirit of gentleness and gratitude. I also integrate patience, mindfulness, and precision into all that I do. I am persistent to the point that I never quit when I have a goal, because I *know* I will eventually reach that goal. Also, generosity is so prevalent in my life that I am highly tuned into finding ways I can help and encourage others wherever I go. And one thing I really love is that my language and thoughts are in sync with my values and belief system—more than ever. With all these principles working together in my life, I now feel I am capable of almost effortlessly, positively impacting other people, and I have so much unleashed personal power that it surprises even me sometimes."

Godfrey beamed. "Maya was right: she said you had magnificent potential, and that it was only a matter of time before you would be a powerful influence for good in the world. She would be proud."

Royce smiled. "Thank you, it's an honor to hear that from you. And yet . . . I know this sounds strange, Godfrey, but I feel I haven't even come close to fulfilling my God-given potential. I *want* to use my gifts even more, but I don't know how or where to start. It seems overwhelming, and at this point I just don't know where to put my focus each day." He paused, took a deep breath, then asked, "But Godfrey . . . what does all this all have to do with you being 'led' here to be with me?"

Godfrey smiled broadly. "It has *everything* to do with it. Seems like the timing of our meeting is perfect—which isn't surprising."

Royce's forehead crinkled in perplexity as Godfrey began to explain.

"A little earlier, when we talked about the plane crash you were almost in, you pointed out that even when people have deeply impactful experiences, there is a tendency later in life to forget the lessons they learned during that moment of crisis. I believe Americans refer to it as 'foxhole religion.' "

Royce nodded and smiled.

"Well, even though *The Six Principles of Sacred Power* is an undeniably spiritual and potentially life-transforming manuscript, given we are mere mortals, there is still the chance or even the tendency for us book owners to waiver or slip into losing our emphasis on the powerful message. That is something Mr. Gandhi would never have wanted to happen. So, after five years of living out the principles, although Mahatma was by then deceased, the surviving men from around the world reassembled and created what we called the Four Daily Pillars of Wisdom."

Fascinated by what he was hearing, Royce wore an expression that prompted Godfrey to continue.

"Essentially, we compared notes on how the Six Principles had manifested most deeply in our lives over those first five years. Then we distilled the common denominators of our experience into four daily choices that we would consciously agree to make, which would thus assure that we continued to embody the overarching spirit of the Six Principles. Although many of us go back and reread the entirety of *The Six Principles of Sacred Power* on a regular basis, the Four Pillars can be recited quickly each morning, and the affirmations continually remind us of the heart of the principles. I guess you could think of it as a daily booster shot," Godfrey added with a grin.

"Sounds like a brilliant idea," Royce eagerly responded. "I am all about keeping it simple."

Godfrey nodded and continued, "Simplicity was an important element of Mr. Gandhi's philosophy, as you may know. As far as the meeting went, I mentioned earlier today that I only attended one of the group's reunions; this was the one. We assembled secretly in Panaji, on the north coast of India. There was a great amount of discussion and prayer on which key tenets would be most representative of the spirit of *The Six Principles of Sacred Power* before we came to a consensus on the Four Pillars. Since that time, when an owner of the book reaches the five-year mark, a more senior member of the group is assigned by Maya to teach that person the daily pillars."

"I absolutely love it," Royce replied with a hearty smile.

"Excellent," Godfrey responded quickly, "because I am going to share them with you tonight."

Royce was stunned. "Godfrey, this is fantastic! The Four Pillars seem to be exactly what I need at this point in my journey."

"Yes, it is time; after all, it's been five years, Royce. Maya personally asked me to share these with you, and I told her I was honored to do so. But keep in mind, as with the ownership of your copy of *The Six Principles of Sacred Power*, you will be one of only a handful of people in the world with this knowledge. There is power in these Four Pillars, not unlike with the Six Principles themselves."

"I'm grateful . . . and I'm ready, Godfrey," Royce said eagerly.

Godfrey smiled with approval.

At that moment, there was a deafening clap of thunder, and the entire hotel went dark, making the wind howling outside suddenly seem even louder. Yet neither man flinched as the electricity went off. And as if each knew what the other would do next, Royce calmly reached over and removed the now useless lamp sitting on the small table between them, while simultaneously, Godfrey located one of the short, thick candles they had placed on the floor, lit it with a match, and placed it on the table in a small decorative bowl.

In the flickering light, Godfrey coughed another deep, hoarse cough, inhaled, and simply stated, "Let's begin."

CHAPTER 8

As Godfrey started the lesson, he reached down and gently removed his stunning ruby ring. Holding it up in the candlelight, he glanced at Royce, then looked down at the inscription. "I assume you saw this earlier," he said with a grin.

"Yes: 'six-five-four,' " Royce said with a look of curiosity. "I wondered. . ."

"Six principles, five years, four pillars," Godfrey replied evenly.

"Of course." Royce lightly tapped his forehead.

"Each man on the original leadership team received a ring at the five-year mark, when we gathered in Panaji. Like *The Six Principles of Sacred Power*, the ring may be passed on to an heir. The ring was—and still is—representative of the oath and the sacred responsibilities held by each book owner," Godfrey added.

Royce's thoughts immediately went back to the necklace Maya was wearing on the morning she left Georgia for India. Come to think of it, the ruby had looked identical to the one in Godfrey's ring. "Ah—and Maya had her father's ring made into a necklace!"

"Yes," Godfrey acknowledged.

"So, Godfrey . . . I already have a question."

Godfrey smiled. "Yes, yes . . . Maya told me you are full of questions."

"Well, she was right," Royce said with a laugh. "But my first question is actually more of a comment: I thought all of the original members of the leadership team were, well . . . deceased." Royce managed to get out.

With a hearty laugh, Godfrey said, "Well, as you can see, that is a bit of an exaggeration. But I must admit, I am the last man standing, so to speak. Sadly, everyone else is gone. And as I shared with you earlier, I was forced to disappear, due to the British putting a price on my head for funding the movement."

Royce interrupted, "They'd come after you even after all this time?"

Godfrey shrugged. "Maybe. The rascals essentially still blame me for having their 'jewel in the crown' taken away all those years ago. They maintain that without the funding I provided—or that they strongly *believe* I provided—the Indian resistance would never have succeeded. I am likely low on their priority list of fugitives these days, but I have no doubt I still am on the list. Regardless, I've quietly gotten to enjoy a little—no, a lot—of island time on Antigua over all these years."

"Ah, playing a little high-stakes hide-and-seek with the British government while right under their noses, huh?"

"If you are referring to Antigua still being part of the British empire, you are correct," replied Godfrey with a smile. "I think the government believes I would never be foolish enough to go into hiding on British soil. What they don't know won't hurt them," he said with a wink.

"So far, so good for you," added Royce with a grin. "So . . . the other members have all passed away. Maya shared with me that each member was allowed to pass on their personal copy of *The Six Principles of Sacred Power* to an heir of their choice. Where do the other heirs live who have been granted the honor of receiving the book?"

Godfrey replied, "As I mentioned earlier, my travels on this adventure have taken me to Morocco, Switzerland, Greece, India, China, and Hawaii. The heirs are living in those places, and so I was blessed to meet with each of them on this trip. Finding them all wasn't easy . . . but the beauty of it was that each person I met greeted me like a long-lost brother."

As the torrential rain continued to batter the hotel, Royce sat quietly in the flickering shadow of the candle, absorbing all that Godfrey had just shared.

Godfrey finally broke the silence, quietly saying, "Let's begin with your instruction, my good man. You have important lessons to learn."

Royce nodded as Godfrey carefully yet confidently began his training in the Four Pillars.

"Each day when you arise, Royce, you'll recite these affirmations I am about to pass on to you. At first it will just feel rote, but trust me, the power embedded in these words is unique. Each pillar has magnificent strength in it—strength for you, and for others.

"Pillar number one is:

" 'Today, I will choose to respond in peace, no matter what challenges occur in my life.' "

Royce thoughtfully rubbed his chin. "Seems easy enough," he said in a nonchalant tone.

"Yes, of course it does," Godfrey said with a laugh. "We are sitting in a beautiful hotel, on a beautiful island, surrounded by peaceful conditions—well, at least *inside* the hotel." He grinned. "The challenge begins when we leave this hotel and are soon thrust into adverse circumstances, or when people treat us in ways we don't want to be treated. Can we easily choose peace *then*? I would offer that only the strongest among us can."

Royce thought back to *The Six Principles of Sacred Power*. "I remember when Maya shared with me the Principle of Supreme Gentleness. She reminded me that the great masters were able to stay gentle even when times were especially harsh. I assume it's a similar concept."

"True. Habitually choosing peace has roots in the Principle of Supreme Gentleness," replied Godfrey. "For example, as you know, it is quite simple to be kind to those that are kind to us—yet to be kind to the *un*kind, well, that is on a different level. A true spiritual warrior knows their happiness is not contingent on the reaction of another person. Happiness is self-generated, and it cannot be taken away—unless we allow that to happen."

"Without a doubt," agreed Royce.

Godfrey continued, "However, this pillar also has a deep connection with the Principle of Unending Appreciation."

Royce thought for a moment. "I think I can see that. If one is in a state of constant appreciation, it would be difficult—if not impossible—to not also be at peace."

"Correct," Godfrey confirmed. "Peace and gratitude are two sides of the same coin. I would venture to say that anyone you know who embodies the trait of deep gratitude is also a deeply peaceful person. I know it's certainly true of the people in my world," he concluded.

"I also tend to associate peace with calm," Royce chimed in. "Aren't they pretty much the same?"

Godfrey paused and thought about the question. "I suppose that if someone is outwardly calm, one would assume that person to be internally peaceful. But peace is the result of going *beyond* mere calm. In fact, some people seem calm on the surface, but they are angry, resentful, or agitated underneath. Once a person has achieved a state of genuine peace in their lives, the calm is no longer just surface level; it is fully baked in, so to speak, and they become nearly imperturbable. Mr. Gandhi was an excellent example of that."

"Are you saying a peaceful person doesn't ever get angry?" Royce asked.

"Not at all, Royce. A person who has learned the art of peace as we define it here—and remember, we are referring to a high level of mastery—has reached a point where it becomes extremely difficult to anger them, that is true. But more importantly, if they do feel angry, that anger is not released in a harmful or negative way; it results in constructive resolutions. Not necessarily a 'happy' resolution, but one that is well thought out and ends up being the best solution possible."

"Sounds like there is very little impulsivity on the part of a peaceful person," offered Royce.

"You're right," replied Godfrey. "That lack of impulsivity is the result of much soul-searching in terms of understanding the core of one's anger. Most often, our anger, like so many negative emotions, is based in insecurity, typically a fear of being hurt or invalidated. But a master of peace has become so supremely confident in their own abilities that there is little insecurity in them. They don't need to be perceived as being right, perfect, or having all the answers, because they believe in themselves, and so they aren't dependent on approval or recognition. The most important thing to them is preserving their state of peace. Therefore, there is little to get angry about—and certainly little to be *impulsively* angry about. You could say they are at peace with themselves, which enables them to easily be at peace with others."

Royce nodded in agreement. "That makes sense to me. In fact, it reminds me of a story, which taught me that lesson very well. When I was younger, there was a long time where I was a struggling author. But I was putting my heart and soul into my writing, and I eventually got to a point where I felt like I was starting to make a difference in people's lives. My sales were getting better, and the book reviews were encouraging. Each day, I would wake up and check the most recent reviews to see how people were receiving my work, and it gave me a lot of happiness to see my budding success.

"Then I got my first poor review—and as crazy as it sounds, it was devastating. I felt so unappreciated and misunderstood that all I wanted to do was strike back at them. Then I received another bad one . . . then it seemed like I was getting a bad review every week! Even though I was still getting mostly excellent reviews, I was starting to see hateful words and comments show up that really were simply mean-spirited."

Godfrey smiled in a gentle, understanding way as Royce continued.

"Just when I got to where I wasn't taking those reviews quite as personally, I found that someone had written the most angry, aggressive, anonymous review of one of my books—and me—that I had ever seen. I saw the evaluation early in the morning, and as much as

I tried not to let it bother me, I was crushed; it affected my mood all day.

"Late that afternoon, I was on my way to catch a flight out of town for a speaking engagement. I got in a cab, and my driver was a jovial, kind-spirited Kenyan woman in her early twenties. She wore a bright yellow dress and headdress from her country, and her smile lit up the taxi. She tried to make small talk, but I didn't feel like talking; I was still annoyed about the book review.

"A few minutes out from the airport, she calmly said the strangest thing to me: 'They don't matter, you know.'

"I was shocked. 'Who are you talking about?' I asked her. She laughed. 'The critics. Seems to me like you are letting them get to you—and that's exactly what they want to do.' I was astonished. I asked her, 'How do you know. . . ?' But before I could finish, she stopped me and said, 'Oh, I know. I have been there.' 'Is that so?' I asked her in a doubting tone.

"My skepticism didn't faze her at all, and she replied with a grin, 'Yes, that is so, and I will tell you that constantly trying to please them—or anyone—is a path to misery.'

"Now she *really* had my attention.

"She continued, 'When I left my native country, I was an accomplished violinist. You see, when I was growing up poor in the tribal areas outside of Nairobi, a missionary came to spend time with us. He was remarkably kind, and he had a talent for playing the violin, which he did for us in the evenings. It was soothing and melodic, and I just knew I wanted to be able to do the same thing for people someday. When he left, he generously gifted me his magnificent violin, which had been given to him in Austria. I practiced day and night. After a few years, I nervously began playing on the streets in Nairobi—and the people there were so kind to me, and so lavish with their praise of my music! One day, I was fortuitously asked to play in a music hall in front of thousands of people. When I finished, they all stood and cheered. But the next morning in the newspapers, the critics were horrible. They called me names and said I should just go back to my tribe—even though most people at the concert had obviously loved my performance.'

"My jaw dropped. 'Just like with me! The naysayers did the same thing to you!'

"She smiled and continued, 'True, but this is the difference: it did not matter to me what the critics said. I believed so much in myself and in bringing people happiness with my music that I could choose not to care about their criticism. I did not need their approval, and I knew if I ever felt like I needed it, I would be a prisoner to that approval—and to them—forever. That was not something I intended to become. In fact, I pressed on with my dream, and eventually I received a scholarship to one of the most prestigious music schools in the U.S., right here in the city. Now I attend school during the day, and I drive my taxi in the evenings to support myself until I finish school. Then I will play professionally . . . and,' she said with a smile, 'the critics still won't like me.'

Royce appeared pensive as he concluded, "Like so many other impactful interactions that occurred in my life before I knew about the Six Principles, I didn't fully understand the synchronistic significance of that event—but I certainly understood the message she was sharing with me. When I got out of the cab, I knew I would never see her again, but thanks to her, I felt like a weight had been lifted off me . . . and I have never looked at my negative reviews since."

Godfrey smiled and chimed in, "That's an excellent lesson indeed, my good man—one I believe we could all benefit from."

Royce paused briefly and then added, "Godfrey, the more I think about it, the more I can see why this would be one of the carefully chosen pillars. Choosing peace can have powerful ripple effects throughout our life, and eventually in the lives of others. And I love how you brought it all back to our own insecurity, which is exactly what my problem was that day I met the African woman. We often believe our anger or frustration is justified because we feel we have been wronged, so we must react or stand up to the perceived villain—but that just perpetuates the cycle. It empowers the critic, and it disempowers us. It's kind of crazy to allow our detractors to have that kind of control over us and our self-esteem, when you think about it."

"Exactly, Royce!" Godfrey cheered. "In these cases, what matters most to a spiritual warrior is living out what we have control over— and a sense of peace is one of the fundamental things we can control."

Royce laughed. "Silly me. I forgot the depth of *The Six Principles of Sacred Power*. I should have known that a simple affirmation about choosing peace wouldn't be so easy to live out."

"Well," Godfrey countered, "Even though choosing peace isn't always easy, it really *is* simple. Most people just choose to make it complicated. Having the courage to live by our core values isn't particularly hard . . . until the ego gets involved. When we feel the need to protect that, well, you're right: things can get complicated."

Royce nodded.

"Okay, good buddy," said Godfrey, "let's take a little break and check out the storm. Then I'll share the next pillar with you; it's one I think you'll particularly appreciate."

CHAPTER 9

Stepping over to the window near the bar, Royce and Godfrey could see the silhouettes of the large palms blowing erratically in the wet, warm night air. "The winds have picked up," Godfrey pointed out. "I'm guessing they are around seventy or eighty miles an hour at this point."

Royce agreed, reflecting on the speed of the sign that had previously hurtled past them.

"All that hot air reminds me of a bloke I knew back in London. He could talk your ear off," Godfrey said with a laugh. "Let's get back to the lesson at hand, what do you say?"

"Sounds good," said Royce. He couldn't help but grab the bag of chips as he sat down for his schooling. He felt like a little boy with his snack, sitting in the front row of a riveting movie.

Godfrey wasted no time. "The second Pillar is this:

" 'Today, I will choose to look for and honor the good in every person I meet, realizing each of us is doing the best we possibly can.' "

Having shared the affirmation, Godfrey simply sat quietly while Royce absorbed the words.

After a few seconds, Royce commented, "Reminds me of the Bible verse: 'Judge not, lest ye be judged.' "

"Although I have never thought of that, I can see that there's truth in that analogy," Godfrey responded. "However, it's also important to understand that we are judging people all the time. It's a natural behavior. The problem occurs when we start *acting on* that judgment—because our verdict we are acting on may be inaccurate."

"I think I understand," Royce said.

"It's really about being open-minded, Royce—which is increasingly difficult to do in our society."

"Now, I'm not sure I know what you mean by that," Royce countered.

Godfrey continued, "We are told more and more through the media what clothes to wear, what car to drive, which neighborhood to live in, which school to send the children to. . . It's exhausting, trying to measure up to what we think our lives *should* be like. Plus, we then start consciously or unconsciously projecting that 'should' onto other people. So not only can we not meet the standard we are being told we *need* to meet, but we also then start trying to get others to do the same thing!"

"Ah, I get it now," said Royce.

Godfrey went on, "This great country was built on individuality. Yet we are often squelching that very uniqueness by trying to pigeonhole ourselves and other people into ways of living and being that are based on someone or something else's ideal."

Royce seemed to come alive as he caught on to the spirit of this pillar. "Come to think of it, the most incredible, innovative people in this world have always marched to the beat of their own drummer. Scientists, engineers, inventors, artists, writers. . . The list goes on and on."

"You are right, Royce. But it takes great courage to be ourselves—and it takes courage to cheer others on as they seek their own path," Godfrey added.

" 'Live and let live,' " Royce chimed in.

"Yes, but 'Live and let live' is really the most basic aspect of this. What I am encouraging you as a spiritual seeker to do is to go much further. I would offer that perhaps the motto could be 'Live passionately and authentically, and help others do the same.' Do you see the difference?"

Royce shrugged.

"Royce, do you remember earlier when I shared with you how Mr. Gandhi made me feel valued and appreciated when I first met him that night in Madras?"

"Yes," he replied quickly.

" 'Value' and 'appreciate' are not stagnant terms. They are words of *action*. If I value and appreciate you, I am going to show it by listening, by caring, by displaying sincere interest—by deeply acknowledging your genuine worth with my actions and my words."

Royce nodded in affirmation as Godfrey continued. "So, if I am open to new ideas, new objectives, and new beliefs, and I wholeheartedly and enthusiastically show that candidness, then I am truly living out of a spirit of openness and honoring the good in others. I am creating a space where I allow the possibility that the person or situation I am encountering may hold a key to unlock something that I never knew or understood. If it is a person, it may mean being open to someone who dresses differently than I do, speaks differently than I do, or thinks differently than I do. But when I wholeheartedly honor that person and look for the good in them, I open doors of potential opportunity on many different levels."

"This makes great sense, Godfrey. When a person is living out the Six Principles, they are living out a life of openness; I can see that. They are using tools like patience, gentleness, gratitude, and generosity to maximize the experience of being fully receptive. But what about the part of the affirmation that states, 'each of us is doing the best we possibly can'? Is that really true?"

"It's certainly the premise I begin with when I meet someone," Godfrey said. "If I *don't* take that approach, the doubt and resistance can create a subsequent power-draining effect for each of us. People come from diverse cultures, upbringings, and degrees of struggle; we have no idea what others have been through that has created their current perspective. When they make a choice— one that you or I might not be inclined to make—they are doing so because of the hundreds of thousands of experiences in their lives that have shaped their thinking. It's presumptuous of us to habitually look only through the lens of our own values in analyzing their decisions."

Royce excitedly jumped in. "I'm with you, Godfrey. So, the best thing we can do is to believe in them, enthusiastically allow them to be who they are—and if we are going to facilitate any change in them, it should be through living in a way that resonates with and inspires them."

"Right," Godfrey affirmed. "Trying to change people isn't our job. Not only is attempting to impose our will usually futile, but it may also be that the change we are trying to dictate isn't the right one for *them*. We just don't know the battles they have faced—or are currently facing.

As Godfrey made this comment, a recollection suddenly flashed through Royce's mind, and Godfrey saw the reaction reflected on his face. "Looks like I may have hit a nerve or a memory." He smiled.

Royce smiled back gently. "Yes—a memorable meeting with someone I won't forget."

Godfrey picked up his tea and leaned back. "I do love a good story, mate. Pray tell. . ."

Royce seemed to go back in time as he gazed into the distance and began speaking. "I remember walking through a short, narrow alley after visiting a coffee shop one morning in my hometown, when I saw him standing quietly in the parking lot ahead of me. He was probably six-foot-three, and his tattered jeans and wrinkled blue oxford shirt hung a bit awkwardly on his thin frame. From the shaggy gray beard, I surmised he was in his sixties. I also surmised that he was about to ask me for cash, which I had 'conveniently' just spent the last of on my coffee."

Godfrey settled in and listened with great interest as Royce continued his story.

"Sure enough, as I smiled and nodded hello, he slowly asked, 'Excuse me, buddy, would you buy an old veteran a cup of coffee?' *Well*, I thought, *that was a bit of a twist on the standard request for money*. So, I shared with him my 'I'm out of cash' story. He smiled in a surprisingly understanding way and said, 'No problem. I've just been waiting on my check from the Veterans Administration. They're slow, to say the least.' And he grinned.

"Something was different about this seemingly homeless man—and it wasn't the fact that he was carrying a small briefcase, although that only added to the odd scenario. Suddenly, visions of the lessons I had shared with my daughters when they were younger began popping into my mind—lessons on giving. 'You never know what someone's life has been like,' I would say to them. Yes, it was time to practice what I preached. 'You know, I bet that coffee shop takes credit cards. Come on, let's go grab a cup,' I suggested. And the old veteran grinned again.

"We walked through the alley and ended up back at the little coffee shop. As we strolled in together, I could feel what seemed like every head turning and staring at the unlikely pair we made. We approached the counter, and I said to the mid-twenties-ish barista, 'This gentleman is a veteran, and I'd like to buy him a cup of coffee.' Still feeling all eyes on us, I was thankful that she smiled and didn't miss a beat. 'My father is a veteran, too.' She beamed. 'Thank you for your service.' He didn't minimize it or take the compliment for granted. Instead, he looked her squarely in the eyes and softly said, 'You're welcome, ma'am.'

"I was beginning to feel great compassion for this veteran, and I wondered if he was hungry. 'Pick out whatever you'd like. Lunch is on me,' I said, fully expecting him to place a hearty order. 'No thank you. Coffee is just fine,' he replied without hesitation. I was surprised, to say the least.

"We stepped outside and sat at a small table, then we began sipping our coffee and talking. I asked him what war he'd been in. 'Vietnam,' he said slowly. I had read a lot about the brutality of that war, but not really knowing what to say next, I paused and added, 'I guess I can't even imagine what it was like there.' He seemed to withdraw a bit, as if he'd heard that many times before. Then he firmly replied, 'Neither could I.

I was only nineteen . . . but I learned quickly.' As the soft spring breeze blew across the patio, it seemed to usher in old memories. 'I did some things over there that I'm not proud of, but I guess they had to be done. Either way, those things are done now,' he added with a tone of sadness. His voice trailed off, and his blue eyes grew misty. 'Both of my grandfathers died in the battle of Normandy, and I remember most of the time in Vietnam, I believed I would be the next one to go,' he said quietly.

"The depth of his pain became acutely apparent to me. We talked a bit more and realized we had quite a few acquaintances in common from our rural Georgia hometowns. I couldn't help but think that this could have just as easily been me, had the hand of fate deemed it so. At that moment, the spring air suddenly felt colder.

"An hour passed like mere minutes, and then it was time for me to go on my way. We shook hands, he thanked me for the coffee, and I thanked him for what he had done for our country. Then I left. As I reached the corner of the building and turned to walk back through the alley to my car, I glanced back and saw him opening that small, mysterious briefcase. It contained a single item that he removed with great care: a beautiful old Bible, very worn, which he carefully opened and began reading with a reassuring smile. I smiled too, and I continued to my car, feeling such a connection with this man that I still can't describe it today."

Royce looked at Godfrey and then offered, "When I share this story with people, I suggest that the next veteran they meet—whether they appear homeless, or wealthy, or somewhere in between—they should thank them for their service, maybe even buy them a cup of coffee. Their struggles may be ones we could never imagine or understand. For me, on that glorious spring day, I learned a lesson that left me feeling grateful— grateful for a chance conversation with a vet, which I will never, ever forget."

Godfrey was clearly touched by the story, and he replied, "I think that is a magnificent example of why we want to look for and honor the good in others—a wonderful reminder indeed, my friend."

Royce nodded, then smiled appreciatively.

The time was going by quickly, and Royce was savoring every moment. Occasionally, the two men would stop and listen to the howling winds, but the bulk of their focus was elsewhere that night. There was just too much to talk about to be bothered by the hurricane.

"Godfrey," Royce asked in a caring way, "did you ever have another serious relationship in your life after you and your wife split up?"

The Englishman paused and thoughtfully responded, "There were a few ladies that I spent time with who could have been 'the one' again, I think. But I believed deep down that the movement was my true calling. Besides, with my constant travels to different parts of the world to oversee the company, it just wouldn't have worked out, I'm quite sure."

There was a wistful tone in his voice, so Royce followed up on his question. "Did you *want* it to work out—maybe even to have children?"

Godfrey became a bit distant, then replied, "There are times in my life that I miss having a family; I won't deny that. Christmas and other holidays . . . they are different when one is alone. But that's the path I chose, and on any path, there are obstacles; the days punctuated by loneliness and sadness and second-guessing are probably my biggest hurdles. However, my life has been very rich, and again, I have no complaints. The times I spent with Mr. Gandhi, Livingston, and all the movement leaders in India were priceless—plus, I am grateful to feel that hopefully I have made a small difference in the world. The subsequent lifelong relationships I have fostered have done much to fill the emotional gaps in my life. I wouldn't change a thing, Royce."

"Powerful and clearly authentic words," Royce responded. "I do understand loneliness, as you probably know. My wife died years ago, and I had to learn to see the world differently—as well as learn how the world would see me differently. . ."

Godfrey circled the conversation back around. "Maya told me about that, and I am deeply sorry for your loss." He leaned forward and added gently, "Royce, this is the nature of open-mindedness and nonjudgement. The heartfelt feelings we just shared are the same kinds of deep feelings everyone feels, in their own way, due to the various hurts and events in their lives. Our experiences allow us to have empathy for other people; knowing the pain *we* have felt can be a catalyst for understanding others' pain."

From the look in Royce's eyes, Godfrey knew the younger man understood.

"Royce, you referred earlier to not knowing what battles people are privately fighting."

Royce nodded.

"Well, a truly open-minded, empathetic person doesn't need to know the specifics of another person's battles—unless that person decides to share their battle scars. What they *do* know intuitively is that we have all dealt with painful struggles, and everyone is worthy of compassion and patience. So essentially, these caring souls treat every person the same way: with love, kindness, and understanding—whether they know the person's story or not."

Royce was obviously processing what he had just heard. "Godfrey, doesn't *anyone* annoy you?"

A smile came across the old Englishman's face. "Well, yes, I suppose every now and then. But there is one person specifically. . ."

Royce cocked his head and raised an eyebrow.

"Me," Godfrey replied. "I understand everyone is doing the best they can, and I also understand how important my attitude is in impacting the lives of others. So, when I sense a hint of arrogance in myself, or insensitivity, or impatience with them . . . I get agitated with *myself*."

Royce smiled and responded, "But that's just human nature, I guess."

Godfrey shot back, "Yes, that may be true. . . However, using the excuse 'It's just human nature' has become a bit ineffective for me, considering where I want to be on my spiritual journey. But rather than being too hard on myself when I do falter, I simply admit my shortcoming, acknowledge that I will learn from it, and then I move on. Encouraging my own growth through taking responsibility, learning from my mistakes, and raising my awareness to better respond to the next situation, seems to be a much healthier path than simply shrugging it off as 'just human nature.' "

Godfrey then became quiet, letting his words sink in.

Royce finally spoke. "Thank you, Godfrey. I remember Maya saying that being patient and gentle with *ourselves* is of the utmost importance, and I have come to understand that to be true. When I make mistakes, I have had the tendency to beat myself up. I like your idea of using perceived mistakes as growth opportunities, rather than dwelling on how I 'failed.' The more I reflect on it, I believe what you are saying is that in the same way we want to avoid harshly judging others, we also want to avoid harshly judging ourselves."

Godfrey nodded and smiled. "Well said, my friend."

With an appreciative look, Royce concluded, "Looking for and honoring the good in others is a concept that I can see would truly represent the spirit of *The Six Principles of Sacred Power*. It's another pillar that was perfectly chosen, in my opinion."

"I agree," said Godfrey. He smiled, then looked down at his watch and added, "I also see that time is marching on quickly tonight; it's already after midnight. Let's take a break for a few moments, then we will keep going. You've done well absorbing the teachings so far, and I have no doubt you'll quickly soak up the next lesson also . . . although the next pillar is one that many people find difficult to put into practice."

Royce sat silently as Godfrey stood and walked over to the window, coughing now in a way that sounded much, much worse than before.

CHAPTER 10

The two men once again peered out the window into the rain-lashed courtyard of the hotel. Royce couldn't help but reminisce. When the children were small, he and his wife would bring them to the hotel for summer vacations. The young couple would play with their daughters in this very courtyard, making up games as the little girls squealed with delight. The sun was warm, life was perfect, and the island felt like an eternal paradise for their little family. . .

Royce's unspoiled vision was shattered by a jagged blinding light. With a deafening crack, lightning struck a large palm before their very eyes, taking down the century-old tree in seconds. Reflexively, he grabbed Godfrey and pulled the older man away from the window. Godfrey, shaken, looked out at the fallen tree and quietly said, "Thank you, Royce. It's intimidating how quickly things can come to an end, isn't it?"

Royce smiled in an understanding way, then guided the pensive man back to his chair. "Yes, it is, Godfrey."

As the two men returned to their seats, each opened a bottle of water, and Godfrey continued his teaching of the Four Pillars. "Pillar number three is this:

" 'Today, I will choose to greet each situation with courage, knowing that everything I want and need lies in overcoming my fears.' "

"This pillar especially hits home for me," Godfrey offered.

Royce was listening intently, even though fatigue was setting in from his long day of travel and the stress of the storm. "What do you mean, Godfrey? I would think courage would come easily to you, with all of your business acumen."

"Well, I would remind you that I took over the business from my father when I was only in my thirties. I never considered myself to be a brave person—or even a businessman. But as I said, I had a great deal of persistence and determination." Godfrey seemed to be reliving those days as he went on, "I remember courage being a trait that Mr. Gandhi showed at all times. There may have been plenty of times when he was afraid—in fact, I'm sure there were—but he pushed through the fear. It never held him back . . . and that's one of the things that made him incredibly special."

"I can't imagine Gandhi being afraid," Royce said in a tone of disbelief.

Godfrey laughed. "I couldn't imagine him *not* being afraid. Think of what and who he was facing: the entire British army and government! The odds of succeeding must have felt insurmountable at times."

"Yes, well, when you put it that way. . ." Royce grinned.

Godfrey replied quickly, "There's no other way to put it. It was something that seemed like an impossible task to most people . . . but not to him. Between his innate courage and the strength he'd gained from *The Six Principles of Sacred Power*, Mr. Gandhi sometimes joked that he felt bad for the British because the odds were stacked against *them*!"

"Turns out he was right," added Royce with a smile.

"Yes, indeed, my good man. But remember, Royce, Mahatma was only a man, just like us. His courage was a choice. It was a choice that ultimately changed the world—but it was one that had to be made, which he did with great esteem. The lesson being, we have access to that same type of courage every day, and it is a fundamental ingredient of greatness, whoever we are and whatever we wish to do."

"An excellent reminder," Royce applauded.

"Yes," replied Godfrey. "However, even though courage is available to us, it is often not put into action, because . . . well, I don't know why, actually. Maybe because it takes so much courage to have courage," he said with a smile.

"Good point . . . I think." Royce laughed.

Godfrey continued, "But seriously, Royce, Mr. Gandhi was an inspiration in many ways, and his courage was certainly one of them. What's more, the courage he showed spread among his followers, and it seemed as if each of these 'ordinary' men was transformed into a man with the fearlessness of a samurai warrior. This courage spread like wildfire through the population. I will say, however, that each of the six men already had lives and careers and challenges that demanded courage, before they ever came to be part of the movement. Their time with Mr. Gandhi simply elevated that courage to a new level."

Royce nodded in agreement, then Godfrey added, "Another thing about courage is that one who is truly courageous doesn't need to boast about how fearless they are; their actions speak for themselves. Maya's father was a wonderful example of that."

"Really?" Royce asked with keen interest.

"Absolutely. There were times when I saw Livingston remain totally calm when a normal person would have been terrified. For instance, when the British were searching for the leaders of the movement—and their families—they approached Livingston for information. He simply and serenely let them know he had no idea where they were, when sometimes the men were hiding just a couple feet away. I think Livingston had ice water in his veins."

"Amazing," Royce said with admiration.

"Yes, and he selflessly demonstrated courageous actions again and again—never uttering a word about his deeds to anyone," added Godfrey.

"I must admit I've never felt like a courageous person," Royce said hesitantly.

"Most brave people say that same thing," Godfrey replied. "I remember Maya saying those very words to me, shortly after her father passed away. She wondered if she would have the courage to not only go on, but to go on with the valor with which Livingston had lived. But, as I shared with her then, courage isn't a feeling; it's an action. When a typical person is labeled a hero for performing a life-saving deed, they often say, 'I don't really feel like I'm anything special.' Ironically, it's true—and not true. It's true in the sense that anyone could have done it. But it's not true, in that the person *is* special, because they *chose* to perform that feat."

Royce pondered Godfrey's words. "So, they still *feel* fear—but they act despite the fear. I guess I could make a courageous decision like that if I had to, especially after everything I have learned from *The Six Principles of Sacred Power*. But those types of decisions don't need to be made very often, so I'm not sure how I would practice courage on an ongoing basis."

"Royce," Godfrey said with a laugh, "the opportunities are everywhere, big and small—and you are practicing courage every day, whether you realize it or not!"

Royce raised an eyebrow, as if he wasn't too sure about that.

Godfrey continued, "The small, consistent decisions to be courageous are almost more difficult than the seemingly big decisions. Making the choice to rescue a person in danger is essentially an instinctive reaction;

most of us would likely do it, I would hope. But the small choices we face each day, like whether to be generous, whether to hold off on making disparaging comments, whether to live honorably and gratefully—these are courageous decisions that most people find it all too easy to avoid."

As if a lightbulb had just gone off in his head, Royce commented, "I've never thought of it like that!"

"It's true, Royce—and when you choose wisely, those daily choices slowly but surely mold you into a person of courage who is ultimately capable of incredible acts of bravery. Not only that; those actions do not go unnoticed by others. The Six Principles, as you know, have an inherently contagious effect on the people around you. Courage is the same way."

"I love it," said Royce. "It really does seem as if it's just a matter of taking the courageous approach in every 'little' situation, which builds a courageous spirit that is able to take brave action in bigger situations—almost automatically."

"You're correct," agreed Godfrey. "The beauty of it is that even if one has a history of making poor choices, or at least choices that were not courageous, one can begin anew at any time they choose, rebuilding their courage 'muscle' quickly and effectively—with results that will make a tremendous difference in their own lives and the lives of others."

Royce smiled. "Another perfectly chosen pillar."

Godfrey nodded, then added, "Royce, let me finish our discussion on courage by sharing this with you. Much of my earlier life, I was plagued by doubt, fear, and a lack of courage. I wish I had understood that small decisions of valor are like making small investments in a savings account: they would add up quickly and serve me well in the future. It would have made situations like taking over my father's business much easier and more seamless. Yet once I did understand this 'magic' compounding formula of courageous choices, I became a changed man. Even now, as I face this dreadful disease, I have the courage and strength to face it, which I never would have thought possible in my early days. Learn from my delay in understanding this powerful knowledge, and the results will serve you well."

As Royce heard these poignant, potent words, he was once again reminded of the gift he was receiving just by being in the presence of Godfrey Tillman. "Thank you, Godfrey. I'm grateful," he gently replied.

"It's my pleasure," Godfrey said with a smile. "Let's take a short break now. It will be dawn before long; our time together is running out quickly, and we still have one more pillar to cover."

CHAPTER 11

After a few minutes of walking cautiously around the darkened first floor to stretch a bit, both men ended up back at the large window. As they looked outside, it was apparent that the weather was only worsening.

"I didn't think it could get any darker," Royce nervously offered.

"It can always get darker, my friend. But then again, darkness is only temporary. The sun eventually returns—always has, and always will," replied Godfrey with a soothing smile.

Royce nodded slowly, then started to speak. But his words were lost in a series of loud, raspy coughs from his companion. He noticed Godfrey quickly reaching into his jacket pocket and pulling out a small white handkerchief, which he coughed into, then wiped it across his mouth. As he removed the cloth from his lips, Royce was taken aback by the small crimson stain that had appeared on the fabric.

"Godfrey, are you . . . okay?"

"It's all part of the plan; I have no complaints," he commented softly.

Royce couldn't help but remember that Maya had uttered those words when she initially told him she would be returning to India. He felt a sick feeling in the pit of his stomach.

Godfrey looked at Royce as if nothing had occurred, somehow summoning a strong voice. "Pillar number four is:

" 'Today, I will choose to trust that everything that happens in my life is designed to make me a stronger, wiser, more compassionate person.' "

"I guess your comment about 'part of the plan' is right on time, Godfrey," Royce said with a forced, slight smile.

"Accepting that life is happening exactly as it is supposed to happen isn't always easy or pleasant, Royce. However, I would say this pillar is as representative of a strong, trusting spiritual life as anything I know. When one is habitually living out the Six Principles, one evolves into a person who trusts—*deeply* trusts—that everything is happening as it should. When that occurs, not only is a new level of strength reached, but a new level of freedom."

Royce smiled again. "Precisely what Maya shared with me, Godfrey. I have to admit, it was hard to grasp . . . but once I was able to trust the plan, my life changed in a way I could scarcely have dreamed."

Godfrey gazed at Royce with a look of admiration. "I can't tell you how good it makes me feel to hear you say that, Royce. God has a plan, most people would agree—but what most people *wouldn't* agree on is the fact that they need to let go and allow the plan to unfold."

"So, why would *you* say trusting is so important?" Royce persisted.

Godfrey rubbed his chin. "Interesting question, Royce. I will say this: We are all going to end up where we are ultimately supposed to be, I believe. However, we can get there by taking a lot of detours and unnecessary side roads, or we can get there by taking a direct course—which is the route of faith. The more we can be in alignment with that route, the more it feels we are 'in the flow,' as they say—and the more efficiently we will make it to our proper destination."

Royce had a puzzled look, so Godfrey added, "Look at it this way, Royce. We are given free will, as you know. However, we can use that free will to attempt to live in sync with God's will for us, or we can use that free will to do whatever feels good in the moment. Now don't get me wrong; I am not saying we should have a puritan mentality, where life becomes strict and boring. I am saying that if we want to get the most out of life, there is a spiritual current running through the world that we can latch onto, which will provide us with energy and abundance without all the stress and resistance. That current is God's plan for us."

"So, how do we find this 'current'—this plan?"

"Well, you fell right into that one," Godfrey said with a laugh. "That's the perfect question. We find it by consistently *choosing* to believe that God is working on our behalf, regardless of how situations appear. This really ties in beautifully with the pillars of peace, courage, and honoring the good in others. When those three pillars are in place, and we then add this mentality of unshakable trust, spiritual blockages diminish. We become dialed into whatever path God has chosen for us, and at that point, miraculous transformations can occur."

Royce thought deeply, then commented, "It just sounds so logical—and powerful. It's baffling that everyone wouldn't choose this course."

"Yes, it's all actually quite simple—but most people insist on making it complicated. There is something in each of us that does not want to give up control over our lives. What most people don't realize is that when they choose to give up control, it is *their choice*, so it's not like something is being taken away from them. Again, it goes back to the free will we have been given. We can freely hold on and try to do it all ourselves, or we can freely let go and allow a wondrous plan to unfold, engineered by the master designer of all plans in the universe. I don't know about you, but I'll take option B any day." Godfrey laughed.

"Amen to that, Godfrey," Royce said with a big smile. "Have you always been fully trusting in your life?"

"Certainly not," he replied quickly. "But I suppose my faith increased as I spent time with others who had that trust—that undeniable, obvious lifestyle built around the belief that everything was going to work out for their greatest good."

Royce nodded. "I felt that way around Maya," he interjected.

"Yes, hers is an excellent example of a lifestyle of pure faith. I believe each of the people who have been directly exposed to *The Six Principles of Sacred Power* has the deep belief that all is going precisely as it should. Of course, as those people have been around other people, that attitudinal ripple effect continues outward."

"Absolutely true. I have seen it happen again and again over these last five years," Royce wholeheartedly agreed.

"Royce, this is why our mission of empowering other people is so important. We live in a world that is hurting deeply, and most of the time, we aren't even aware of the hurt all around us. We are so tightly bound to the problems and fears in our own lives that we fail to see others' pain—even as we pass them and look into their eyes. But we can change all that and help heal this desperate planet. It's what all the great spiritual teachers Gandhi studied were trying to teach us. I wish I had understood sooner, on many levels. . ."

Royce tried to soothe the pain the memories seemed to be bringing back. "We all have regrets, Godfrey," he said softly. "You did the best you could."

Godfrey smiled. "It sounds odd, but it's not particularly a regret; I know regrets only make matters worse. It's more of a wish that I had understood how powerful the principles were early on. Yes, of course I would have liked to spare myself a lot of the pain I suffered . . . but more importantly, I could have helped so many more people."

"Your deep desire to help people is inspiring," replied Royce. "How did you come to fully understand the importance of generosity? From your time with Mr. Gandhi?"

Godfrey shrugged. "Maybe. I have to say that when I first met him at the cottage that night in Madras, I sensed generosity and compassion in him to a degree that I had never experienced. Then when I read *The Six Principles of Sacred Power*, everything came together. The generosity element seemed to resonate with me at a higher level than anything else. I felt that trait was incredibly powerful in helping others—and in healing ourselves. My connection with this principle took my benevolence to a point far greater than it had ever been—even though most people already believed I had a magnanimous spirit."

Royce thought for a moment. It was interesting to hear these words from Godfrey. Although many people would have thought him boastful, Royce knew he was simply relaying his experience in a way he felt simply to be factual—and he was clearly correct.

"My faith has always helped guide me to be generous," Royce added. "And I also have altruistic parents. As I was growing up, I saw in them a great love for people, and I wanted to be the same way. My daughters have exhibited that same type of compassion, so hopefully I have also passed it on to them. In the same way you connected with the focus on generosity in *The Six Principles of Sacred Power*, I did as well."

Godfrey was listening carefully. "Royce, I have no doubt your children are generous. It would be impossible for them to be any other way—especially after being around you post-Six Principles. Share with me a time when you saw that spirit in them."

Royce didn't have to think long before he came up with an example. "One day I was at a restaurant with my oldest daughter, Becky—I think she was twelve or thirteen at the time. We were sitting at the front of the eatery, and she was facing a large window. As we were talking, I noticed she kept looking over my shoulder, until suddenly she blurted out, 'I'm sorry, Daddy, but he needs help!' I didn't understand, but as I turned to look out the window, my daughter jumped up and ran outside. Watching her carefully, I saw her walk over to an apparently homeless man, probably in his seventies, who was bent over going through a trash can. Becky walked up and spoke to him. Then she reached into the pocket of her jeans and took out the twenty dollars of allowance I had given her only hours before. She smiled and handed him the cash. The man immediately began sobbing, and he reached down and hugged my daughter.

"As far as pure compassion goes, that scene was unlike anything I had ever seen. When she walked back into the restaurant, I asked her what she had said to the man. She simply replied, 'I just asked him if I could help, and he politely said, 'No, thank you.' But I knew I couldn't be happy until I *did* help him—so I gave him my allowance. I think you would call that a great investment, right, Daddy?' she said with a smile."

Godfrey smiled approvingly and commented, "I think that is a splendid example of the power of generosity. You can be grateful your daughter came to understand this concept at such an early age. In these days of so much entitlement and selfishness, it is an increasingly rare story to hear about children performing generous acts. The parents' focus nowadays seems to more often be on their children's achievements, rather than on their children making a difference in the lives of others."

Royce nodded his agreement.

"When we have this mentality of sharing, it enables the natural unfolding of our lives," Godfrey went on. "When we aren't fighting to get more, do more, or be more, we can simply relax, live peacefully, and trust in God's bigger and better plan—which is what this pillar of total trust is all about. Generosity is tied to it all."

Godfrey paused, then added, "Royce, the pillars of wisdom I have shared with you tonight are loaded with power. However, it is important to remember that the pillars themselves—although they have the spirit of the Six Principles woven into them—have no power unless we *believe*. Without this, the pillars are only empty words . . . but I don't need to remind you, as I am sure Maya instilled that in you very well." Godfrey smiled.

Royce grinned. "You can say that again. That's a lesson she wasn't going to let me forget. By the way, Godfrey, speaking of Maya, how much time were you able to spend with Maya's family over the years? Were you able to get to know them outside of the business of the movement?"

Godfrey nodded. "Livingston and I became close. I think a large part of it was the fact that we both were from England, but aside from that, we realized early on that we had so much else in common. I spent quite a bit of time in their family home in New Delhi over the years, and I got to know each of the family members well—including Maya. At that time, she was in her twenties, but I knew that she was already a very special young woman. In fact, I had no doubt she would impact the world—which she obviously has done on many levels."

Royce chimed in, "I certainly can attest to that. I feel immeasurably blessed that I was able to meet her and spend those days with her in the gardens years ago. She truly changed my life—and even more powerfully, she taught *me* how to change my life."

Godfrey agreed. "One of Maya's gifts is to bring confidence back into people's lives. I saw it happen many times—and her father was the same way. I remember when my wife left, I had so many doubts and so much pain, but Livingston helped me put myself back together."

"I had my own demons to fight," Royce volunteered. "I think understanding *The Six Principles of Sacred Power* helped me realize I didn't have to be a prisoner to those feelings. I was deeply impacted by my own tragedy, of course, but I came to understand that I did not have to be *defined* by what happened to me."

"Well put," Godfrey affirmed.

At that moment, a fierce gust of wind burst violently through the nearby window, showering the room with shards of glass, and plunging them back into darkness. The force of it was so strong that it tossed the furniture around, knocking the two of them to the floor.

Royce sensed it was now or never. "Godfrey! We've got to get out of here—let's go!" he shouted.

Godfrey unsteadily nodded his agreement. "But where can we go?" he attempted to yell over the torrential rain now blowing into the room in sheets.

"I know of a small storm cellar, tucked away on the other side of the property behind the old housekeeping staff quarters," Royce managed to get out. "My children discovered it one day when they were playing on the grounds. It's only about two minutes away, if we can make it there. . . ."

Godfrey managed a smile as Royce helped him to his feet. "Jolly good idea, Royce! I'm right behind you!"

Royce scrambled out the door on the other side of the bar, with Godfrey close behind. The wind seemed to taunt them with blood-curdling screams as the two men reached the stairs outside the hotel—almost as if the storm were daring them to try to cross the grounds. Royce plunged forward into the courtyard, the rain beating on him mercilessly. He turned and yelled as best he could over the deafening storm, "Can you make it, Godfrey?"

Godfrey had now fallen a few steps further behind; he was scarcely visible to Royce as sheets of rain swept across the hotel landscape. "Don't mind me, mate. Takes more than a little rain to stop Godfrey Tillman!" he bellowed.

Royce shouted his encouragement back to Godfrey as the men moved slowly but surely toward their destination—now only about a hundred yards away—but his words were drowned out by the whipping winds and torrential downpour. Although he could feel the terror of the storm, he also felt the adrenaline rushing through his veins, creating a surge of euphoria. As he approached the storm cellar burrowed into the ground behind the old home, he turned to Godfrey to declare their victory. "Buddy, we did it!" he proclaimed ecstatically.

But what he saw then filled him with panic. . .

CHAPTER 12

With dawn breaking, there was just enough light to see—but Royce couldn't believe his eyes. Godfrey was about twenty yards behind, on his knees, trying desperately to stand up.

Royce screamed at the top of his lungs, and the winds seemed to blow even stronger. "No! Godfrey!" Sprinting back toward the fallen man, he watched helplessly as Godfrey stared straight ahead blankly, then collapsed onto his back on the soaked ground, eyes shut tight against the pouring rain.

Royce breathlessly knelt and put his hand gently behind Godfrey's neck and head as the man managed to barely open his eyes. Godfrey coughed violently—and this time a thin stream of blood flowed down the side of his mouth.

"Royce," Godfrey managed to utter, "what an honor it has been to spend this night with you."

"Don't speak, Godfrey. I have to get you some help!" Royce frantically used his shirt to wipe the blood from Godfrey's face.

"I have all the help I need, right here," he replied. "I'm sure the roads are blocked from the storm, and my time is near anyway; I wouldn't have it any other way. Now, listen to me. . ."

Royce fought back tears as Godfrey coughed deeply, caught his breath, and spoke. . .

"After the time we have spent together, you know the story of Godfrey Tillman—a young man many years ago, who wanted desperately to be successful. He studied, worked hard at the university, then went into a business he believed could help his family, and provide for many employees and their families."

Royce tried feebly to wipe the driving rain from Godfrey's face as the old man continued.

"He found a woman he deeply loved, then continued on the path he felt he should follow—doing 'big things' in the world." Godfrey coughed loudly and harshly, but continued. "Then one day, he lost the love of his life. He then realized that his focus on what he had thought were the big things, had led him to take for granted what, in hindsight, were the *truly* big things. All of his schooling, all of his hard work, and all of his achievements were nothing . . . compared to what he'd lost."

Godfrey was now gasping for breath, and Royce felt helpless to do anything except allow the man to speak.

"But what is important is this: *that* is not the end of the story—and those who have had a similar experience can learn from this also. The end of the story is that every difficult thing, every painful thing he had ever gone through, had prepared him for what he would share with others later in life. He realized the fire he'd endured would one day help ignite a blaze that would light the way for the ones who so desperately needed it."

Royce nodded, wiping the tears from his own face.

"Remember this, Royce: it is never too late. It's *never* too late to build on what seems like worthless pain, because it is never worthless if we choose to find the gift in it—and that gift is not always obvious at the time. No regrets, just trusting the lessons are ones we need for our journey. . ."

"For sacred warriors like us, it's the only way, Godfrey," Royce gently cut in.

Godfrey smiled faintly, took a deep breath, and offered his hand. "Take my ring, Royce."

"What? What are you talking about, Godfrey?"

"Royce, I knew that one day, I would have a worthy person placed into my life to share the Four Pillars with—and to whom I would pass on the ring. I never doubted that. And I knew after talking with Maya that *you* would be that person. You now know the Four Pillars, and you are more than worthy. The pillars will bring you the strength and wisdom you have been looking for, to carry your mission to the next level. *Your* ring is now a reminder of that."

Hesitantly, Royce slid the ring off Godfrey's finger and put it on his own hand. "Godfrey, I can't begin to explain how blessed I feel to have shared this time with you," he avowed. "When I met Maya and was introduced to *The Six Principles of Sacred Power*, I became the person I'd always had the potential to become. My conversations with you have fanned the flames of that fire in me. Your life and your lessons remind me so much of what I have gone through, and I am a much better man for us having spent this time together." Then his composure crumbled. "What can I do, Godfrey? What can I do to help you?"

Godfrey gasped for breath, then coughed deeply one more time. "Royce, it looks like my trip home to Antigua is going to be exchanged for a different sort of homecoming," he managed with a pained smile. "So, I want you to go to Antigua in my place. There is someone you must meet as part of your own journey."

Royce raised an eyebrow as he immediately blurted out, "What? Who? What are you talking about, Godfrey? I need to meet someone—in the Caribbean . . . ?"

"Royce, if you have learned anything from the Six Principles, the Four Pillars, and the events in your own life, it is to have total faith in the way your life is unfolding to help you make a difference in the world. Don't ask questions, for it will all become clear to you—every step of the way. Just continue to trust. Now more than ever . . ." With that, Godfrey attempted to reach into his jacket—but then his hand abruptly fell limp, and his eyes softly closed.

Royce screamed out into the fury of the storm. "You can't go, Godfrey! You can't leave!"

At that moment, the old gentleman that Royce had known for little more than twelve hours—it seemed like a lifetime—took one last labored breath as every wrinkle dropped out of his rain-soaked face.

Godfrey Tillman, the wise, jovial, self-proclaimed "citizen of the world" . . . was now a citizen of the great world beyond.

CHAPTER 13

Against all odds, a young man carrying what appeared to be a small black medical bag came running through the downpour. When he reached Royce, he saw him cradling Godfrey's limp body.

"I came as quickly as I could," he said apologetically. "I barely heard the shouting over the storm; I'm staying at a small guest house on the east side of the hotel grounds. I thought I was the only one still on the property! I'm a doctor, and I didn't know if there might be some way for me to help, so I decided to stay. I've called for an ambulance, but I have no idea when they will be able to get here with this storm. I don't even know if the bridge is passable."

Noticing a bit of blood still on Godfrey's face, the doctor immediately checked for a pulse. After a few seconds, the young man shook his head and turned to Royce with a telling look of sadness and compassion.

It was unimaginable. Royce's life since he met Maya had been one remarkable "coincidence" after another—although he grasped now more than ever that there were truly no coincidences in life. Meeting Godfrey Tillman had been yet another incredible synchronicity, but he also intuitively knew that the lessons he had learned from Godfrey were just the beginning, as far as what this relationship meant to Royce's future—and maybe to the lives of many others. Silently, he reflected on the irony of how his trip to Jekyll Island had yielded the exact answers he was looking for—but in a way he could never have foreseen. It was another example of how Maya's teachings years ago on unwavering trust had once again become manifest in his life.

Strangely, at that moment, the wind began to die down. The howling of the storm steadily diminished, as did the driving rain. In the distance, Royce could now hear the wailing siren of the coming ambulance.

Still gently touching Godfrey, as if to somehow stay connected to his fallen mentor, a visibly shaken Royce watched in silence as the ambulance pulled up and two paramedics rushed over to them.

"I'm sorry," they both said, almost in unison.

One of them regretfully explained, "When we got the call from Dr. Broward here, we left as quickly as we could. At first, we couldn't even see three feet in front of us through the storm. But for whatever reason, right before the eye was to come across Jekyll, the hurricane took another erratic turn—only this time it went back out to sea. When the winds and rain started letting up, we were able to get across the bridge—just not soon enough. . ."

Just then, Royce looked up and saw that the hotel manager had arrived. "I'm sorry for your loss, Mr. Holloway," he said, clearly distraught. "These types of storms are so rare on Jekyll. I've lived here all my life, and this is the first hurricane I have ever experienced. It was . . . horrible."

Royce stood and nodded, then looked around at the scattered debris. Surprisingly, the damage paled in comparison to his memory of the aftermath of Hurricane Frederic. "How bad is the damage to the hotel?" he asked.

"For a hurricane like this, we're lucky it wasn't far worse than it was. From what I am hearing already, other parts of the island suffered tremendous loss. But the hotel overall was spared—just some broken windows, a lost sign, a few downed trees, and a huge amount of wash from the rain."

The other paramedic then gestured to Godfrey and asked Royce, "Are you a relative of this gentleman?"

The question struck Royce as odd. In the short period of time he had spent with Godfrey, the two men had become like brothers. "No," Royce answered gently. "It just . . . seemed that way."

The paramedics and the doctor looked at Royce, as if they somehow knew what he meant. But Royce was certain they couldn't possibly know—because even *he* didn't understand how a relationship like this could have formed in such a brief time.

Royce felt the tears running down his face mix with the steamy Southern drizzle as he watched the medics lift the gurney now carrying Godfrey's body into the ambulance. As the men started to pull the doors shut, Royce's mind suddenly and intuitively flashed to Godfrey's last action: the attempt to reach into his jacket.

"Wait!" he shouted in an adamant tone. Rushing over to the vehicle, he calmly yet firmly said, "Please look inside his jacket. I think he had something there for me."

The paramedics looked quizzically at Royce, but one of them reached into Godfrey's blue jacket. Sure enough, he pulled out a small envelope with the name ROYCE scribbled on it.

"Yes," Royce offered. "That's for me." The man nodded and handed the envelope to Royce, closed the doors, then silently motioned to the driver.

Once the ambulance pulled away, Royce slowly walked back up to his room, sat down at a small table, then carefully opened the envelope and began reading the enclosed letter.

Royce,

My good man, I felt sure this time might come soon, and if you are reading this, my intuition was correct.

Knowing you as I already feel I do, I am sure you will want to help with my final arrangements.

However, I would ask that you refrain from worrying about this, since things are already being handled as you read this message.

As I have now shared with you, I would like you to travel to my beloved home island of Antigua. There is an extremely important lesson waiting for you there—one that will not only impact your life, but will also potentially impact people throughout the world.

Your contact will be my housekeeper, Suzanne Dismont. You will find she is a special woman, to say the least, and I have trusted her for many years without question. You can do the same. Her number is on the back of this letter, and she will take care of all your travel arrangements—at no expense to you, of course.

Safe travels and good luck, Royce. The world is indeed a much better place because of the gifts you so compassionately share with others. Soon, those gifts will change more lives than ever. . .

Namaste, my friend,
Godfrey

Looking up from the letter, Royce felt a variety of emotions, including deep sadness over losing Godfrey, and immense interest as to what possibilities the man had envisioned for his chosen student.

Slowly, Royce reached for the phone and dialed the number written on the back of the letter. Miraculously, even with the storm damage on the island, the call seemed to be going through. One ring, then another, then another. . .

Finally, a woman with a soft, measured Caribbean accent answered. ". . . Mr. Holloway?"

"Yes," Royce replied apprehensively.

"I'm Suzanne Dismont—I've been expecting your call. I'm grateful you have chosen to honor Mr. Tillman's request; I somehow knew you would."

Royce paused, his palms becoming sweaty, and he felt himself trying to speak. But the woman continued, and her words only added to his speechlessness.

"Mr. Holloway, your driver will meet you at the Jekyll Island Club Hotel today at four o'clock to take you to the airport."

Royce's head was spinning. He couldn't understand how all of this had happened—especially how it happened so *quickly*.

What he did understand was that his vacation plans to spend the next few days in coastal Georgia had suddenly changed.

Standing up, breathing slowly and deeply as he calmly gathered his courage in a way that would have made Godfrey Tillman proud, Royce firmly replied, "I will *definitely* be ready."

Royce Holloway . . . was headed to Antigua.

The Four Daily
Pillars of Wisdom

- *Today, I will choose to respond in peace, no matter what challenges occur in my life.*

- *Today, I will choose to look for and honor the good in every person I meet, realizing each of us is doing the best we possibly can.*

- *Today, I will choose to greet each situation with courage, knowing that everything I want and need lies in overcoming my fears.*

- *Today, I will choose to trust that everything that happens in my life is designed to make me a stronger, wiser, more compassionate person.*

AUTHOR'S NOTES

The Gentleman's Journey is based on a short story I wrote, simply titled "The Gentleman." It was a true story about an older man I met one summer evening sitting at the bar of the Jekyll Island Club Hotel (which in 2017 was renamed the Jekyll Island Club Resort)—in the same way and in the same place where Royce Holloway meets Godfrey Tillman.

There are many elements in the short story and the book that are true. For example, the conversation I had with "the gentleman" started out exactly as it does in the book. As I sat down and looked up at the golf tournament on the television, we both watched Tiger Woods sink a magnificent putt, and he shouted out a comment about how great Tiger Woods is. That simple remark ignited a fascinating conversation that lasted for hours.

Like Godfrey Tillman, this gentleman had been diagnosed with a terminal illness, and he was on a month-long trip down the coast to rest up before his experimental surgery. I met him on a Saturday on the last leg of his trip, and he said Jekyll Island just "seemed like it would be a nice place to stop and relax."

Also, like Godfrey, this gentleman was divorced and had no family. He candidly elaborated on this with me, and his comments were almost word for word what Godfrey says in the book when Royce asks him about traveling alone.

We had lots in common. Among other things, we were both business owners, we liked the same type of books, we traveled to the same types of places, and we enjoyed the same foods. The more we talked, the more we realized how similar the paths we'd traveled in our lives had really been. The conversation flowed effortlessly, as if we were long-lost friends, and I loved every minute of it. As we wrapped up our time together, we exchanged contact information, then heartily shook hands, vowing to connect again during the days ahead. He put on his tweed derby hat, tipped it at me, and then with an easy smile, he turned and walked away, disappearing into the warm, humid Jekyll Island night.

A few days later, I returned home and called to wish him good luck with his treatment. He thanked me, and we talked of getting together as his recovery allowed. He said he would be in touch. But as with many relationships forged during travel, it seems it wasn't meant to be. As the days and weeks went by, I realized our time together had likely faded, like the sun setting over the soft, colorful edges of the coastal horizon the evening I'd met him. Maybe that was just the way it was supposed to be: two people sharing a powerful, comforting experience of spiritual synchronicity, but one which was never meant to last forever.

Yet even if I never see him again, I will always remember sitting down next to "the gentleman," and I'll relish those hours when our paths crossed on that fateful summer evening on Jekyll Island.

Wherever you are, thank you, my friend. . .
I'm mighty grateful you touched my life.

—Skip

ABOUT SKIP JOHNSON

Skip Johnson is an inspirational author and speaker whose goal is to encourage and empower his audience to live happier, more successful lives.

As a business leader, Skip practices what he preaches on attitude and happiness. In helping to run his family's health club chain in Georgia for thirty-five years, Skip helped steer the clubs to earn numerous national and international awards, including Best Customer Service Club Worldwide out of more than seven hundred locations, awarded by Gold's Gym International in 2000.

Skip received a BA in political science from the University of West Georgia. He is also the author of the inspirational books *The Mystic's Gift* (Book 1 in the Royce Holloway series), *Grateful for Everything*, and *Hidden Jewels of Happiness*.

Skip is an accomplished storyteller, best known for his motivational and educational talks that focus on exploring leaders' potential to influence culture and increase happiness. He has also earned the designation of Master Tennis Professional, held by less than one percent of sixteen thousand international tennis professionals certified by the United States Professional Tennis Association.

Skip lives outside of Atlanta, Georgia, with his wife, Anne Marie.

To read Skip's other books, e-books, and articles, or to join his readers' group to keep up with his latest writings, visit www.skipjohnsonauthor.com.

For daily inspiration, you can find him on Facebook at www.facebook.com/SkipJohnsonAuthor.

CAN I ASK A FAVOR?

Thank you for reading my book! Would you do me a favor and take a moment to write a short review on Amazon? Reviews are so important to authors like me, and if you would share your thoughts so others can find out about my writing, I would be truly grateful.

If you leave a review, feel free to let me know by dropping me an email at: skipjohnsonauthor1@gmail.com so I can thank you personally!